EVOLUTION

WHERE DO MUSLIMS STAND?

SYED ASLAM
B.Sc. Honors, M.Sc., Patna University
M.S.,Eastern Michigan University

First Edition
2010

Publisher
The Muslim Observer
29004 West 8 mile Rd.
Farmington MI 48336

Cover, see page 54

ISBN 978-1-4507-1952-0

Printed in USA
Diggy Pod LLC

Dedicated to

Allama Muhammad Iqbal

CONTENTS

ACKNOWLEDGMENTS

Thanks to my Turkish-American friend, Mr. Edip Yuksel, for letting me publish his article on Mr. Yahya in this book; and for providing me first hand information about him. I am obliged to Dr. Abdul Rahman Nakadar for the encouragement and for publishing my articles and rebuttals in The Muslim Observer on the subject of evolution. Those articles became the base for this book. I am thankful to my friend Muhammad Omair for reading the manuscript and for his various suggestions. I want to thank my son, Faiz S Aslam, and my grandson, Aakif S Aslam, for their technical help in shaping this book. I am thankful to Dr. T. O. Shanavas, author of *Creation and/or Evolution an Islamic Perspective,* for providing some references about Mr. Harun Yahya and The Institute of Creation Research, a Christian creationists group. I am obliged to my brother-in-law Mr. Syed W Jafry for reading the manuscript. I am grateful to my artist sister, Sofia Taj, for all the drawings and the design of the cover of this book. Thanks to my daughter Shazia and my niece Raina Karim for reading the manuscript. In the end, I must thank my wife Shahnaz Aslam for her encouragement and support.

FOREWORD

Evolution is a touchy subject for some Muslims, though it should not be that way. Syed Aslam is trying to reconcile a scientific fact with Islamic concept of creation. In the first chapter of the book he argues passionately that evolutionary concept is not in contradiction with the Qur'an. Many *ayahs* of the Qur'an which he has quoted in this chapter do not oppose the idea of evolution; rather they all seem to support it. In the second chapter he discusses how giant intellectuals of the past like Al Jahis, Al Biruni, Jalaluddin Rumi, Al Tusi, and Ibn Khaldun argued for evolution, though scientific knowledge was still in the state of infancy in those days. In the same chapter he also shows that modern thinkers like Sir Syed Ahmed, Allama Muhammad Iqbal, Dr. Muhammad Hamidullah, and Dr. Israr Ahmad were ardent supporters of the theory of evolution.

In chapters three through nine Mr. Aslam has discussed the scientific fact about evolution. Without having much scientific background I can clearly understand his argument, because Mr. Aslam has written this book so that even the lay person can understand the meaning of evolution. He has devoted six chapters to prove that evolution is a fact. You do not need a scientific background to understand how old our planet earth is and why in each geological strata we have fossils of only certain types of creatures. And as you move up in geological time period you see the changes and improvements in the fossils of the organisms. No scientific background is required to understand the predictive power of the theory of evolution and to see how transitional fossils, vestiges, atavism, and embryology all point towards the validity of evolution. The eleventh chapter, in which he has tried to prove the evolutionary processes on molecular basis, is a little technical, but it is quite comprehensible. Some Muslims think that believing in evolution is a sin. Mr. Aslam has turned around the argument by saying that if Allah has chosen the path of evolution to create everything on Earth, then will denying that truth make Allah happy? The Qur'an says again and again not to hide the truth. In the last chapter, much to my delight, he has challenged Mr. Harun Yahya –which was long overdue. I am glad and honored to write the foreword for Mr. Aslam's book "*Evolution: Where Do Muslims Stand?*"

Dr. Syed Husain Majid

INTRODUCTION

Three years ago I came across an article written by Harun Yahya in *The Muslim Observer* on the theory of evolution which was full of misinformation. I had a discussion about the article with Dr. A. R. Nakadar, CEO of *The Muslim Observer.* He suggested to me that I write a rebuttal which I did. My rebuttal was very well received by the readers and I received several e-mails in favor of my article. I even got an invitation from one brother, a professor, to write a book on evolution with Islamic Perspective. I agreed and started reading books on the related subjects when I came across a reference of the book: *Creation and / or Evolution an Islamic Perspective* written by Dr. T O Shanavas. I purchased the book and after reading it, I gave up the idea of writing another book on the same subject. No doubt, Dr. Shanavas has done an excellent job of explaining and covering the topic. I found out that he lives in Michigan, so I invited him to my house and had a long talk on the subject of evolution with him and my other friends. We decided to write articles on the subject of evolution for *The Muslim Observer* and we published seven such articles in the paper on different aspects of evolution. All the articles were well received by the readers.

The main reason why I changed my mind and decided to write this book is to confront people like Mr. Harun Yahya, who is propagating Christian creationist agenda in the Muslim world. He has succeeded to some extent, in creating doubt among some Muslims that the theory of evolution has a corrupting influence on the Islamic culture which is coming from the West. This has promoted a profound anti-science attitude among some Muslims which certainly is not going to help the Muslim countries to catch up with the developed world, in science and technology. He is doing so on a massive scale. It is clear that Yahya's project commands an immense amount of financial resources. It is doubtful that Yahya's lavishly produced materials support themselves, they are priced below market value, and obtaining them even for free takes no great effort. Yahya's web sites make most of his books available on line, in a wide variety of languages at no charge at all. Turkish creationist has gone international, and Yahya's books are as easily found and as prominently displayed in Islamic bookstores in London, Chicago, and all big cities of the Muslim world. The organization behind all of this is known to some extent but the sources of its finances, are virtually unknown. About two years ago he spent more than a million dollars to distribute his voluminous book free of cost to university professors all over Europe and United States.

It is really frightening that this college dropout, a high school graduate, is setting the educational course of the Islamic world in science. You can judge his intellectual maturity and knowledge by reading his interview taken by James Adil of *The Muslim Observer* in 2009.

> **Adil:** You argue very passionately to refute the theory of evolution and you have made it very clear the importance evolution plays as a pillar of unbelief. But

there has been a backlash from secular Muslims such as Syed Aslam and Mike Ghouse, who have been published in our newspaper and who seem singularly determined to attack your arguments, and who try to argue that belief in creationism is simply founded in insecurity and unwillingness to leave traditional or unscientific beliefs. Please give a response specifically to Muslims who try to advocate evolution and try to paint it green.

Yahya: Ask these people how the angels and jinns were created. Will they be able to say they came into being through evolution? No, of course they will not. Or ask them if they can account in terms of evolution for how the Prophet Musa's (as) staff turned into a fully formed snake with digestive, motor and reproductive systems when he threw it down on the ground. When the Prophet Jesus (as) breathed on a bird-shaped object made out of mud, it turned into a living, flying bird. How do they explain that?

The fact is that behind the efforts of some Muslims to reconcile Islam and evolution in their own eyes, lies an element of ignorance and an element of defeatism, a fear of being unable to respond to Darwinism. These people imagine, with the knowledge of the 1900s, that evolution is a scientific theory and that opposing evolution means opposing science. But they are unaware that science refutes evolution. Evolution is a theory unable to explain even how a single protein came into being by chance, a theory at a complete dead-end. Moreover, not one of the 100 million fossils unearthed confirms evolutionists' claims. Darwin admits that himself, saying,

"Why, if species have descended from other species by insensibly fine gradations, do we not everywhere see innumerable transitional forms? Why is not all nature in confusion instead of the species being, as we see them, well defined? Everything is highly regular and perfect", he says. Because Allah creates them, that is why. "But, as by this theory innumerable transitional forms must have existed, why do we not find them embedded in countless numbers in the crust of the earth?"

Because evolution never happened, that is why. Does that not finish Darwinism right from the outset? There are 100 million fossils and they all prove Creation. So can one speak of Darwinism under such circumstances?

Adil: What do you believe would be the effect in the Muslim community of widespread belief in evolution?

Yahya: There is no longer any possibility of that. Because I have proved the invalidity of evolution with very clear, manifest, scientific, technical and irrefutable evidence. People now smile when they listen to someone talking about evolution. The Islamic world is much more aware on this subject, Insha Allah, and apart from a few people deficient in knowledge, the Islamic world is now well aware of the kind of corruption Darwinism really is. Darwinism is a pagan religion. It is a primitive idea that goes back to Sumerian times. It is a heretical, abnormal religion that deifies matter (Allah is surely beyond that) and ascribes divine power to atoms with their own unwise acts. It has nothing to do with science. In paleontology and geology we investigate the strata of the earth and learn how creation took place. We examine those 100 million fossils one by one. And we compare them with living things today. And we see they have never changed at all, that there is no difference between living things' earliest and final forms. That is science. But when we look at Darwinism, all we see is fantastical tales from start to finish. We ask how protein came into being. Darwinism says by chance. We ask how the cell came into being. Again by chance, it says. So how did the cell develop? How did organs emerge? How did human beings start to see? And hear and speak? All by chance, it says. Is chance science? Of course, not. In short, Darwinism is a heretical, imaginary religion

> entirely based on chance, with absolutely nothing to do with science. It is a manifest deception. It is clear that Muslims should not be taken in by such a deception.

Look at the arrogance, ignorance and immaturity of Mr Yahya refuting the work and effort of thousands of outstanding scientists in almost every branch of science who support evolution. As usual Mr. Yahya misquoted what Darwin had said in his book *The Origin of Species.* The quotation mentioned above about Darwin in his interview is completely wrong. He repeats like a parrot the same thing again and again that scientists have refuted evolution and that the fossil of the transitional species has not been found. Both claims are incorrect, propagated by the Christian creationists which Mr. Yahya repeats. I responded promptly to his interview which is included in this book. I also found out what exactly Darwin had said in his book about the transitional species. Darwin said in his book *The Origin of Species*:

> The main cause, however, of innumerable intermediate links not now occurring everywhere throughout nature depends on the very process of natural selection, through which new varieties continually take the places of and exterminate their parent-forms. But just in proportion as this process of extermination has acted on an enormous scale, so must the number of intermediate varieties, which have formerly existed on the earth, be truly enormous. Why then is not every geological formation and every stratum full of such intermediate links? Geology assuredly does not reveal any such finely graduated organic chain; and this, perhaps, is the most obvious and gravest objection which can be urged against my theory. The explanation lies, as I believe, in the extreme imperfection of the geological record[1]

Darwin was an intelligent and an honest man, so he mentioned the weakness of his theory. He was correct that the geology and science in general was in developmental stage at that time. But his prediction was correct --now the paleontologists have unearthed thousands of intermediate species which Darwin was looking for; not only that, the theory of evolution has been proved on molecular basis.

Michael Shermer an American writer and philosopher once said:

> Darwin matters because evolution matters Evolution matters because science matters. Science matters because it is the preeminent story of our age , an epic saga about who we are, where we came from, and where we are going.

To me also, both evolution and science matter, and that's why in the first part of my book I have tried to prove by irrefutable facts that evolution is not just a theory but it is also an undeniable fact. I don't believe in atheistic evolution, who thinks life came on earth as a matter of chance and so human beings are also the product of chance. I see the evolutionary process theistically. I find a great grandeur and beauty on how Allah created this world of ours, step by step and left the signs (*ayah*) for us to decipher it. Everything has been created by Allah in stages, which Qur'an repeats again and again. We sow a seed, the seed grows into a tiny tree and then slowly matures into a big tree giving flowers and fruits. Nothing in this world happens in an instant.

Look at our own intellectual evolutionary process. We first passed through the Stone Age then by year 3000 BC came the Bronze Age which continued for another 2000 years. In about 1200 BC we discovered iron and since then the Iron Age is upon us. We passed through the age of rudimentary guns to fast firing automatic guns to fighter plane to advanced rocketry. At present we are in the computer age or call it the information age. In the last six thousand years we human beings have evolved intellectually by leaps and bounds which no one can deny.

Believe it or not we humans are still evolving and shall go on evolving. Have you ever thought why our brothers in Africa who live near the Equator have jet black skin color and kinky hair? No, not because God cursed them as some white people believed, rather they are blessed by God to protect them from the scorching sun light and ultraviolet rays. Similarly the Nordic people who live near the North Pole have a white color and blond hair because of similar reasons --cold and soft sunshine. Don't go very far; examine your own set of teeth. Study only a ten thousand year old human skeleton and you will find a set of 32 teeth including the four wisdom teeth in every jaw. Now human beings are gradually losing their wisdom teeth[2] with some individuals having them congenitally absent. If it happens to come out sometime after the age of 17 years most of the time it has to be extracted, why, because our jaws are shrinking, and there isn't enough room in our jaws to accommodate those poor wisdom teeth.[3] But why our jaws are shrinking? Because we are not eating rough and tough food any more, we are eating softer and softer food every day and if we go on doing this, chances are that we may lose even more teeth. Why? Evolution is at work, use it or lose it. How about our canine teeth? Is it not the vestigial residue of very old ancestors? Look at the cave dweller fishes and salamanders where it is pitch dark, both of them have lost their eyes for the same reason, use it or lose it because the gene for maintaining the eye is turned off.

There are many evidences to support the theory of evolution which I have discussed in the first part of the book. The present century is going to be the century of biology and evolution is the bedrock of biology, nothing makes sense without it in biology. Yet there are many educated Muslims who are scared by the word, *evolution* and they think that just reading about it will weaken their faith. I hope my book shall calm them down and strengthen their faith by finding the truth. Qur'an places a very strong emphasis on empiricism (Seek knowledge by observation). Truth and knowledge are the only way of attaining closeness to Allah; lies and deceit have no place in Islam.

The last part of the book is about Mr. Harun Yahya, people should know who Harun Yahya is and where he is coming from and what damage he is doing. We educated Muslims have the moral obligation to confront these people and to present the truth to our youth. Though it may appear as if I was projecting myself as David and him as Goliath but that does not matter --truth shall prevail. It also includes the article written on Yahya by other people, who know Yahya first hand. For the interest of the readers I have included my rebuttals to Mr.Yahya's articles on evolution published in *The Muslim Observer.*

1

EVOLUTION AND THE QUR'AN

There is a debate going on between the Christian Creationists and the larger scientific community about how life came on the earth. The Christian creationists believe that life on earth was created spontaneously by God some six to seven thousand years ago in seven days. The genesis leaves no room to manipulate the idea of old earth theory. In contrast to the Book of Genesis, Qur'an does not use a day by day chronological description, instead the Qur'an uses concise terms which do not contradict the idea of old earth. *Where a day the measure of which is fifty thousand years.* (70:4)

Institute of Creation Research (ICR) and Intelligent Design, though both are two different sides of the same coin have recruited a few half-baked scientists to twist the scientific fact and are trying very hard to derail the theory of evolution. Their main aim is to confuse general public, and capture classroom of America to teach Bible version of story of creation.

While this debate is going on, many Muslims are wondering where we stand on this issue. Some in the Muslim community like the Harun Yahya are acting like the agent of Institute of Creation Research (ICR) and promoting the Christian Creationist agenda by writing books and publishing articles borrowed from (ICR) in Muslim news papers. As Muslim scientists, it is our obligation to confront this misinformation and try to present the truth to our young Muslim students. We cannot bury our heads in the sand and pretend that all the overwhelming scientific facts do not exist or tell our children that when you study biology or biochemistry do not study the chapter on evolution. As I see it, we don't have to bury our heads in the sand; the Islamic conception of creation is compatible with the theory of evolution as we shall see when we examine our holy book the Qur'an. As a matter of fact finding compatibility with the scientific theory is in the interest of Islam, because our Muslim children caught between the stiff and dogmatic opposition from the Mullah and finding irrefutable scientific evidence will face a huge dilemma. This way they will have no conflict between science and Islam when they grow up and attend schools and universities.

There is a strong need to reconcile reason with revelation. We Muslims, are already behind in science and technology. The twenty first century is going to be the century of biology. Evolution is the bedrock and the cornerstone of modern biology. It unites all the fields of biology under one theoretical umbrella. Nothing makes sense in biology without the concept of evolution. If Muslims en mass reject evolution it will make the chances of Muslims catching up in science even more remote.

Muslims have already suffered a lot by the ideas of Imam Hanbal(d 855 CE), al-Ash'ri (d 936 CE) and al-Ghazali, an Islamic thinker of the twelfth century who condemned brilliant Muslim scientists like al-Kindi, Ibn Sina and al-Farabi and many others as heretics. His powerful writings shut the door of *Ijtehad* (Innovation) and scientific thinking in the Muslim world and plunged the Ummah from one of the most splendid eras of human creativity to the Dark Ages.

Some educated Muslims think that even reading the article about evolution will weaken their faith in Islam. Is our faith that weak? I don't think so. Islam is a religion that encourages the followers to use their intellect and knowledge to attain the ultimate truth (*Haqq*). This Quranic verse conforms to that logic:

Lo! Man is in a state of loss, save those who believe and do good works and exhort one another to ***truth*** *and exhort one another to endurance. (Qur'an 107, 103)*

As a matter of fact to deny the truth is to deny Allah. There is no theological or logical basis for excluding God's use of natural processes to create living creatures including us. Betting against science is a losing proposition for any religion, be it Muslim or Christian. The idea that acquisition of knowledge will weaken their faith is so depressing to me, because it shuts your brain off. That exactly what we Muslims are practicing for the last six hundred years and the result is in-front of us. Does God dwell in the shadows of our understanding? Or should we be able to find Him in the bright light of spiritual and scientific knowledge?

Should we Muslims behave like Middle Age Christian Popes who persecuted Galileo and burnt Bruno (Italian astronomer) alive (1600 CE) for going against the teachings of the Church that earth is flat and is the center of the universe? They are the same white Christians who believed that black people are half human, just because they are black and different from them. By denying the truth are we not putting our self in the same predicament as the Catholic church of the Middle Ages?

If we study the Qur'an carefully we will find that it strongly commands the believer to use his or her God-given intelligence to understand the universe, its elements and the surroundings. The Qur'an says:

Do not the disbelievers see that the heavens and the earth were fused then We ripped them apart and We made every living thing of water? Will they not then believe? (Qur'an21:30)

Qur'an confirms what scientists of today agree upon, which is that the elements in the Universe were created all at once, which is known as the "Big Bang theory":

The Qur'an says:

Say: Travel in the earth, then behold how Allah originated creation, then He produces a later creation: for Allah has power over all thing. (Qur'an 29:20)And in the earth are signs (ayah) for those who have firm faith, and in your own self. Can ye then not see? (Qur'an 51:20-21)

The worst animal before God are the deaf, the dumb, and those who do not use their reason. (Qur'an 8:22)

It is very clear from these verses that the Qur'an is commanding the believer to travel throughout the Earth and discover how Allah created and seek rational knowledge by observation. It is also very obvious that Allah created it in stages *(later creation)* and definitely not in one shot. If you try to explain the verse (51:20, 21) in the modern scientific context you can say that there are signs (Fossils) scattered all over the earth go and study it. Those who are not using reason are the lowest form of beast in the sight of God. Qur'an says again and again: *Don't hide the truth (2:283).* So let us examine the other verses of the Qur'an to see if it is compatible with the idea of evolution. The Qur'an says:

And Allah who has created all dabbah from water. (Qur'an 24: 45, and other places in Qur'an)

The word *dabbah* in Arabic means anything which has life which includes all animals which can walk or crawl on its belly even bacteria. This is exactly what the evolutionists are saying that in binging all life was formed in water from water. Qur'an says:

"What is the matter with you that you fear not the greatness of God, when you see that it is He that has created you in diverse stages?" (Qur'an71:13-14)

Some people interpreted it to be the stages of a fetus in the womb, but there is no reason why it can't be interpreted to mean stages of evolution.

And Allah hath caused you to grow as a growth from the earth (Qur'an 71:17)

The concepts of these two verses are the back bone of the theory of evolution which states that each and every organism evolved in stages and came into existence out of this earth. The word *Khalaqa* has been used in the Qur'an many times pertaining to the creation of human beings and the universe as a whole. According to William Lane the compiler of Arabic- English lexicon, the verb *Khalaqa* means "proportioning a thing into another thing". In other words bringing a thing into existence from other forms. So if we translate the word *Khalaqa* today in English it will definitely be '*evolve*'. The above verse can now be read like this. *He evolved (Khalaqa) you in diverse stages.* The Qur'an says:

He, Who perfected everything that He created - He started the creation of man from clay then he inculcated in him the potential to reproduce through a drop of humble fluid then He embellished and fashioned him in due proportion; and breathed into him of His spirit and developed in you listening, vision and feeling.(Qur'an 32: 7-9) Disbelieves thou in Him Who created thee of dust, then of a drop (of seed) and then fashioned thee a man (18,37)

The above verses are telling us that man was created from the clay of the earth. The 'creation from clay', does not imply that God created a statue of a man from clay and then gave life to it. We can interpret it like this: we all know that clay has life- giving minerals and the presence of water increases the potential for producing life in the clay, so God inculcated the clay with life. Here the Qur'an is not saying how long it took after the first inoculation to create a man like species. This can be considered the first stage of the creation which Qur'an is referring to "He *started the creation of man from clay*".

When a man like species came into existence the first stage and the second stage can be combined to one in which God gave the ability to *reproduce from a drop of humble fluid.* The third stage is very important where God finally *fashioned man in due proportion.* This implies that God shaped our face, our body and everything, which we see in human beings today. At this stage God gave the capacity to listen, to speak, to understand, and then He breathed His spirit into him and thus God created Adam and Eve. If God created a perfect man (Adam and Eve) in one shot then why Qur'an is saying again and again that God created man in diverse stages?

Some say that believing in evolution will lead to immoral behavior, that we are only a intelligent animal, so we will act like animals. In fact we do behave worse than animals. To address this the Qur'an emphasizes in many ayahs that describe humans as members of the animal kingdom, and invite humans to learn from animals:

There is not an animal (that lives) on the earth, nor a being that flies with its wings, that does not form part of communities like you. We have omitted nothing from the Book, and they (all) shall be gathered to their Lord in the end. (6:38) Then God sent a raven, who scratched the ground, to show him how to hide the naked corpse of his brother. "Woe is me!" said he; "Was I not even able to be as this raven, and to hide the naked corpse of my brother?" Then he became full of regrets.(5:31)

Theory of evolution does not belittle man; it elevates him far above any other animals including his nearest relatives. It leads him on the apex of the evolutionary tree, turning him into an ultimate product of evolutionary processes the best and the brightest of His creation. Through the eye of evolution we see the world which is dynamic, and flexible filled with endless variety and intricate beauty. It suggests that we are not propped up by some magic but came through a step by step process where the Creator cared to tell us our story from the rock of the earth itself. The creator through the evolutionary process forged our brains which opened the whole new world. We learned to improve our lives immensely compared to our ancestors who were plagued with diseases and discomfort. No other creature comes close to us even remotely. In the end I do not see any contradictions between the theory of evolution and Qur'anic concept of creation. This is the reason why the early and modern Muslim thinkers and scientists believed in evolution.

2

EVOLUTION AND ISLAMIC THINKERS

It is hard to imagine, but it is true that the early Muslim thinkers believed in evolution. They understood the Qur'anic verses, explore their surroundings, used their intelligence and logic to come to this conclusion. These towering intellectuals were the product of four hundred years of golden age of the Islamic era, which is considered as the most splendid era of human creativity. While the west was in the dark ages, Muslim civilization was producing brilliant scientists like, Al-Jahiz, Ibn Sina, Al Beruni, Ibn Arabi, Ibn Rushd and Ibn Khaloon to name just a few and they were all evolutionists. It is possible that Darwin himself might have conceived the idea of evolution from the works of those Muslim Scientists, because their books were translated into European languages and were taught in their Universities for hundreds of years.

Al-Jahiz (776-868) was the author of many books; *Kitab al-Hayawan* (The book of Animals) is one of his famous works. It is an encyclopedia of seven volumes of poetic descriptions of varieties of animals. Though it is by no means a book of zoology, but it has description of a very keen study of animals and insects. He was the first person who studied the influence of the environment on animals and developed an early theory of evolution. Al-Jahiz considered the effects of the environment on the likelihood of an animal to survive, and thus he became the first person to describe the Struggle for Existence. His idea on the struggle for existence is not very different from Darwin's idea on this subject. In the *Book of Animals* he has summarized it like this;[4]

> Animals engage in a struggle for existence; for resources, to avoid being eaten and to breed. Environmental factors influence organisms to develop new characteristics to ensure survival, thus transforming into new species. Animals that survive to breed can pass on their successful characteristics to the offspring.

The above statement is so wonderfully close to the modern theory of evolution which was put forward more than thousand years before Darwin. Indeed it seems that Darwin took al-Jahiz's idea as a base and formulated the theory of evolution in a more scientific way in the context of nineteenth century scientific knowledge.

Al-Jahiz gave the idea of the food chain He said: that all life depends on each other. Even the hunting animal can become a part of the food chain which he argued keeps a balance in nature and maintains a proper ratio between the animals. He made an attempt to classify the animals in a linear series. He arranged them in groups having marked similarity and then subgroups. He thus sowed the seed of scientific classification of animals.

Ten centuries before Darwin Al- Beruni, (973-1048 AD), one of the brilliant scientists of Islam, also considered to be one of the greatest scientists of all time, explained natural selection in almost the same way as Darwin did. He knew the disparity between reproduction and survival of a species due to structural advantages. He wrote:

> The life of the world depends upon sowing and procreating. Both processes increase in the course of

> time, and this increase is unlimited, while the world is limited. When a class of plant or animal does not increase any more in its structure, it may come into existence once and perish. On the other hand if the plant and animal do increase in structure, they survive and spread all over the earth.
>
> The forester leaves those branches, which he perceives to be excellent, while he cuts away all others. The bees kill those of their kind who only eat, but do no work in their beehive. Nature proceeds in a similar way.

There is very little difference between Darwin's idea of natural selection or the survival of the fittest and Al-Beruni's concept of natural selection.

Encyclopedia *Rasail Ikhwan al-Safa* (Brethren of Purity) a giant compendium of 52 epistles was written some time during the tenth century by unknown writers. The thinkers explained how life on earth developed in successive stages, from minerals to plants to animals and finally to humans:

> The first stage of the plant kingdom is connected with the last stage of minerals and the highest stage of the plant kingdom with the first stage of animal. The highest stage of the animal kingdom is connected with the first stage of humans.

Abu Bakr Mohammed ibn Arabi (1165-1240 AD) who was born in Spain was a brilliant scholar, interpreter of the Qur'an and a Sufi of the first order. His concept of gradual evolution of species is very similar to that of other Muslim scientists of the time. Here he says:

> Then creation continued on earth, minerals, then vegetations, then animals, and man, If man does not reach the stage of perfection, he is an animal man whose appearance resembles the external appearance of man. Here we are concerned with Perfect Man. The first of human species whom God made the Perfect Man was

> Adam. Thus God demonstrated the stages of perfection for the species.

The above ideas of Ibn Arabi clearly demonstrate that Muslim thinkers knew about the existence of hominid species before the emergence of modern man. He makes distinction between the "animal man" and perfect man. God chose the perfect man as intended vicegerent on earth.

Al-Tusi (1201-1274) has written extensively on the subject of biology and he was one of the pioneers of biological evolution.[5] He explained how plants then animals and then humans evolved, he then goes on to explain how hereditary and variability were important factors for biological evolution. He gave this idea 600 years before Darwin in his popular work, *The Nasirean Ethics,* he wrote:

> The organism that can gain the new features faster are more variable. As a result, they gain advantages over other creatures and have a better chance of survival.

Al-Tusi then explains how human beings might have evolved from advanced animals, he says:

> Such advanced animals (apes) live in the Western Sudan and other distant corners of the world. They are close to animals by their habits, deeds and behavior. The human has features that distinguish him from other creatures, but he has other features that unite him with the animal world, all differences between organisms were of the natural origin. The next step will be associated with spiritual perfection, will, observation and knowledge. All these facts prove that the human being is placed on the middle step of the evolutionary stairway.

It is obvious that al-Tusi's view on evolution was very similar to that of Darwin. He presented his idea based on Islamic philosophy that God created the world and then things developed on its own under His guidance.

The famous mystic Persian poet Jalaluddin Rumi (1207-1273 AD) echoes the same theme about evolution of life as other Islamic thinkers. In his philosophical treatise, *Masnawi-ye Ma'nawi* he describes how life came on earth. According to him evolution and the natural selection were acts of God. He wrote in his *Masnawi:*

> He came first to the inorganic realm and from there stepped over to the vegetable kingdom. Living long as a plant, he has no memory of his struggles in the organic realm. Similarly rising from the plant to the animal life he forgets his plant life, retaining only an attraction for which he feels especially in the spring. Then the creator draws him from animality to humanity. So he went from realm to realm until he became rational ,wise and strong.

Ibn Khaldun (1332- 1406 AD) the famous Muslim historiographer, social scientist and naturalist wrote in his masterpiece work, *Muqaddimah,* that life started from minerals to plants to animals and finally to man. Here is the quotation from his book:

> One should then look at the world of creation. It started out from the mineral and progressed, in an ingenious, gradual manner to plant and animal. The last stage of mineral is connected with the first stage of plants, such as herbs and seedless plants. The last stage of plants is connected to the first stage of animals. The animal world then widens, its species become numerous, and, in a gradual process of creation finally leads to man, who is able to think and reflect. The higher stage of man is reached from the world of monkeys, in which both sagacity and perception are found, but which has not reached the stage of actual reflection and thinking. At this point we come to the first stage of man. This is as our (physical) observation extends.

It is very obvious that Ibn Khaldun knew that other hominid species more advanced than the monkey existed though it was not equal to modern man and that modern man evolved from the primitive hominid. Many other famous Muslim thinkers like Ibn Miskawayah (930-1030 AD), Abu Bekr Ibn Tufail (1107 1185AD), and Abu al-Walid Ibn Rushd (1126-1298 AD) had the same view as the above mentioned Islamic thinkers. Why did the Muslim thinkers developed the evolutionary paradigm of the origin of life? Well, it is because they derived their thought from the Qur'an in addition to their keen observation and study of their surroundings.

Modern Muslim Thinkers and Evolution.

Sir Syed Ahmad of India was a contemporary of Darwin and he believed in his 'Theory of Evolution' putting forward the argument that the fall of Adam and Eve was actually a symbol for human beings to distinguish between good and evil[6].

Allama Dr. Muhammad Iqbal the great poet and thinker of Indian Subcontinent, believed that modern science is compatible with Divine consciousness. He considers it more precious than mere belief in God and says that the scientific study of nature, which is what evolution is, brings man closer to God, a kind of mystic search and an act of prayer.

Allama was an ardent supporter of evolution. In his book *Reconstruction of Religious Thought in Islam* he pointed out[7] that the idea of evolution was first presented by Muslim scientists before Darwin. Al-Jahiz (776 –869 CE), the author of *Kitab-al-Haiwanat,* was the first to hint at the changes in animal life caused by migrations and environment. He then mentioned Ibn Maskawaih (942 – 1032 CE), the author of *Fauz al-Asghar*, who gives a clear and in many respects thoroughly modern theory of the origin of man.

Hossein al-Jisr, a Lebanese Scholar who wrote more than twenty five books, including *Al-Risala al-Hamidiyya* and *Falsafa Science and Qur'an* [8], makes efforts to reconcile the theory of evolution with the Qur'anic teachings. He seems to defend Darwinian's theory and quotes the Qur'anic verse "*We made every living thing from water, will they not believe*?" (21:30) and then agrees with the theory of evolution. There is evidence in the Qur'an to suggest that the species, each of which exists by the grace of God, were created in stages.

Dr. Muhammad Hamidullah (1908 - 2002) is a well known Muslim scholar of the Indian subcontinent. He authored 24 books on different aspect of Islam and mastered 22 different languages. He was awarded the highest civilian award of Pakistan; *Hilal-e-Imtiaz*. He fully accommodated the theory of evolution with the Islamic concept of creation. According to Dr. Hamidullah there is no conflict between evolution and Islam; it is simply presumed that Darwin's theory has been rejected by Islam.

He says that the concept of evolution has been discussed in the encyclopaedia *Ikhwan-al-Safa*, "Brethren of Purity" written in 10th century and no Muslim theologian had any objection. In the Qur'an it is stated that God made men out of clay. Our concept of the creation of man is that God, like a potter, moulded clay into shape and breathed his spirit into it and Adam was thus created. He argues, but what does one do with verses 18:37, 22:5, and40:67 which state time and again that God created man from clay and sperm? It is obvious that clay does not create sperm: it comes from an animal and a human being. It means that the mention of all intermediary stages of evolution has been omitted and attention is drawn to the original source, which is clay. The last cause is the sperm of man which stays in the womb of a woman. The Qur'an states, *When He created you in stages* (*Wallah-o-Khalaqaqum Atwara*, 71:14). The word *tawr* is the basis of *tatawwar,* which means evolution. This can also mean that God created man as a mineral in the first instance. Mineral developed into vegetation, which developed into animal life. There is no contradiction between evolution and Qur'anic concept of creation he says.[9]

Dr. Israr Ahmed is a well known Pakistani preacher and scholar of Islam. Dr.Ahmed Afzal a student of Dr. Israr Ahmed wrote a brilliant article entitled "*Qur'an and Human Evolution*". In this article Dr. Afzal has taken the idea and insight of Dr. Israr Ahmed bridging the gulf between theory of special creation and biological evolution. Both scholars believe that evolution is a universal fact which can be established through the study of comparative morphology, paleontology, embryology, genetics and molecular biology.

Dr. Ahmad Afzal has mentioned the fossil record of bipedal human-like forms *Australopithecus*, *Homo habilis*, *Homo erectus* and finally *Homo sapiens* (Modern Man). There is a general agreement regarding the relationship between modern Man and the various man-like hominid mentioned above. A number of anthropological and biochemical studies have pointed the emergence of all present day humans from a small group of individuals, perhaps somewhere in Asia or Africa[10,45]

Both Dr. Ahmed Afzal and Dr. Israr Ahmed believe that when the process of biological evolution reached its goal and the final form of man appeared on earth, Almighty Allah selected a single pair --a male and female and endowed them with their spiritual souls. All other members of this species died and became extinct and that all of us are descendants of this human pair, Adam and Eve. The Qur'an, however, is silent as to when this happened. The modern scientific findings also points in the same direction that all human beings of today are the descendants of a single pair. Because Mitochondrial DNA in each living human being can be traced back to a single female, who lived some 100,000 years ago.[10,45]

3

THE AGE OF THE EARTH

A simple, straightforward reading of the biblical record indicates that the earth was created in six days and only 6000 years ago. Standing in firm opposition to that view was Al-Beruni, a tenth century Muslim thinker and scientist, who rejected the Judeo-Christian interpretation of Genesis. He used the Qur'an and simple logic to estimate that the age of the earth[11] could be more than billions of years old. Lord Kelvin of Glasgow published calculations that fixed the age of Earth between 20 million and 400 million years. He assumed that Earth was formed as a completely molten object, and determined the amount of time it would take for the surface to cool to its present temperature.

With the discovery of radioactivity, radiometric dating methods are being used to determine the age of rocks. Every radioactive element has a half life period which indicates that during that period of time half of the atoms of that element will decay into other element. The half life time of the radioactive element varies from a few seconds to billion years. The element carbon[12] exists in abundance but along with it we also have a very small amount of carbon^{14} which is radioactive. When the organism is alive it is_getting both $C^{12\&14.}$ But upon its death it becomes a time clock. Why, because it is no longer getting.$C^{14.}$ and from the decay of C^{14} present in the sample we can calculate age of that material. This is possible because the rate of decay of C^{14} is known. There are over forty such techniques, each using a different radioactive element. It has become increasingly clear that these radiometric dating techniques agree with each other and as a whole present a coherent picture in which the Earth was created a very long time ago. Further evidence comes from the complete agreement between radiometric dates and other dating methods such as counting tree rings or glacier ice core layers.

The age of Earth cannot be computed directly from material that is solely from the Earth because the processes of erosion and crustal recycling have apparently destroyed the entire earliest surface. The oldest rocks which have been found so far date back to about 3.8 to 3.9 billion years. Some of these rocks are sedimentary, and include minerals which are themselves as old as 4.1 to 4.2 billion years. To determine the true age of the Earth meteorite samples have been used because meteorites are the same material from which our Earth came into existence. Thousands of meteorites, which are fragments of asteroids that fall to Earth have been recovered. These primitive objects provide the best evidence of age for the time of formation of the Solar System. There are more than 70 meteorites of different types, whose ages have been measured using radiometric dating techniques. The results show that the meteorites, and therefore Earth and the Solar System, formed between 4.5 and 4.58 billion years ago[12].

Now that we know the age of Earth, geologists have divided this age into a series of time intervals. These time intervals are not equal in length like the hours in a day.

Instead the time intervals are variable in length. This is because geologic time is divided using significant events in the history of the Earth. For example, the boundary between the Permian and Triassic is marked by a global extinction in which a large percentage of Earth's plant and animal species were eliminated. Another example is the boundary between the Precambrian and the Paleozoic which is marked by the first appearance of animals with hard parts which can fossilize.

Eons are the largest intervals of geologic time and are hundreds of millions of years in duration. In the time scale you can see that the Phanerozoic Eon is the most recent eon which began more than 500 million years ago. Eons are divided into smaller time intervals known as *eras.* In the time scale one can see that the era is divided into three: Cenozoic, Mesozoic and Paleozoic. Very significant events in Earth's history are used to determine the boundaries of the eras.

Eras are subdivided into *periods*. The events that bound the periods are wide-spread in their extent but are not as significant as those which bound the eras. In the time scale you can see that the Paleozoic is subdivided into the Permian, Pennsylvanian, Mississippian, Devonian, Silurian, Ordovician and Cambrian periods. Illustrated on page 28.

Finer subdivisions of time are possible and the periods of the Cenozoic are frequently subdivided into *epochs.* Subdivision of periods into epochs can be done only for the most recent portion of the geologic time scale. This is because older rocks have been buried deeply, intensely deformed and severely modified by long-term earth processes. As a result, the history contained within these rocks cannot be as clearly interpreted.

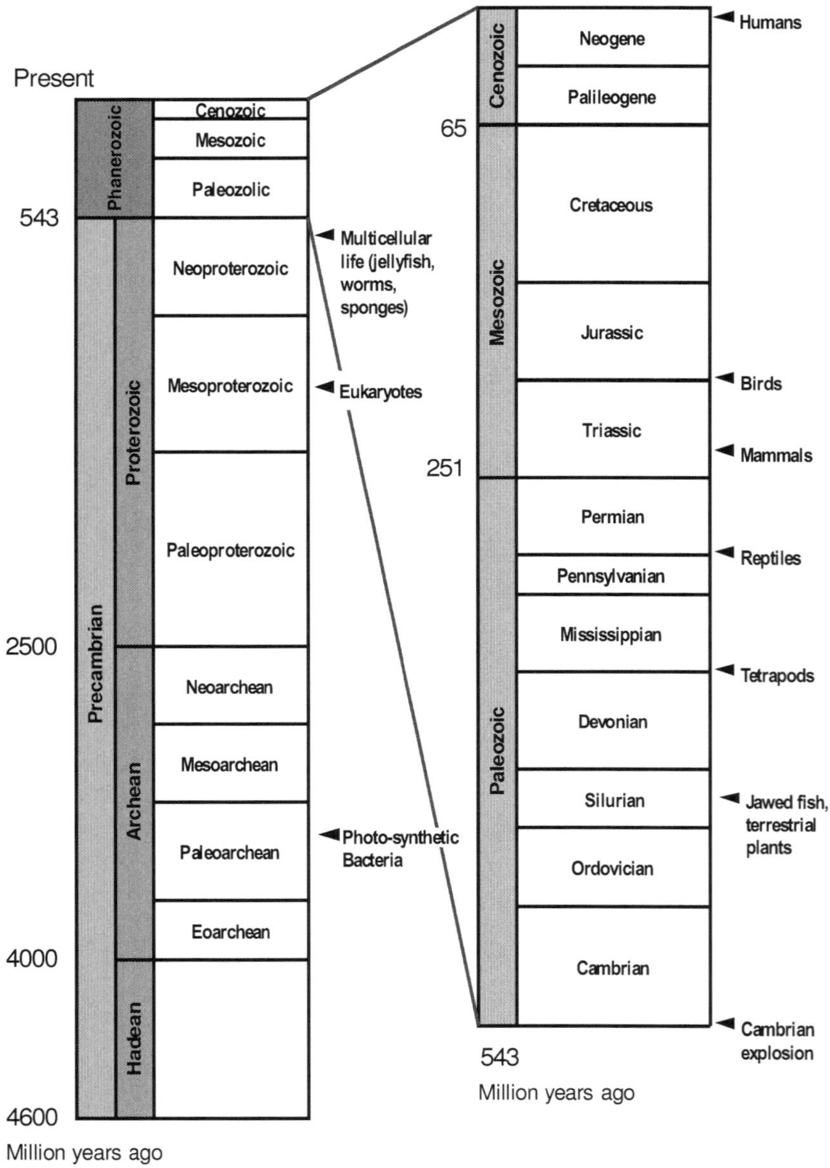

FIGURE 1. Life appeared on Earth in an orderly evolutionary fashion

Continental Drift

A German geologist and meteorologist Alfred Wegener first proposed the theory of continental drift in 1912. According to his theory parts of the Earth's crust slowly drift atop a liquid core. His theory was not accepted for many years -- as late as 1953. In 1958 a geologist Mr. Carey introduced the theory of plate tectonics which provided sufficient geological explanation for the continental drift. Wegener hypothesized that there was a gigantic supercontinent 200 million years ago, which he named *Pangaea*, meaning All-Earth.

Eduard Suess was an Austrian geologist who first realized that there had once been a land bridge connecting South America, Africa, India, Australia, and Antarctica. He named this large land mass Gondwanaland, named after a district in India where the fossil plant *Glossopteris* was found. This was the southern supercontinent formed after Pangaea broke up during the Jurassic period. Suess based his deductions on the fossil plant *Glossopteris*, which is found throughout India, South America, southern Africa, Australia, and Antarctica.

Pangaea started to break up into two smaller supercontinents, called Laurasia and Gondwanaland, during the Jurassic period. By the end of the Cretaceous period, (65 MYA) the continents were separating into land masses that look like our modern-day continents. Continental drift can now be measured by GPS system.

4

WHAT IS EVOLUTION?

According to the Oxford Concise Science Dictionary, evolution is defined as the gradual process by which the present diversity of plant and animal life arose from the earliest and most primitive organisms, which is believed to have been continuing for the past 3000 million years. Evolution is also defined as a gradual process in which something changes into a different and usually more complex or better form. Scientifically speaking evolution can be precisely defined as any change in the frequency of alleles within a gene pool from one generation to the next. As it is most famously used, "evolution" is the process by which an organism becomes more sophisticated over time and in response to its environment and food.

The theory of evolution is a scientific theory, like the theory of gravity, relativity and continental drift. Each of these theories are an explanation that has been confirmed to such a degree, by observation and experimentation, that an educated person accepts it as close to fact in absence of any other theoretical explanation. That is what scientists mean when they talk about a theory: not an unreliable speculation, but an explanatory statement that fits the evidence. The theory of evolution comes under the same category as other major scientific theories, with its explanatory and predictive power; it has become the central organizing principle of modern biology and paleontology. Furthermore, the supporting evidences are abundant, various, and ever-increasing and solidly interconnected. Yet even an educated person some times would say that it is "just a theory" without giving a serious thought. There are various reasons for this: lack of scientific knowledge, unawareness of the overwhelming evidence, rigid religious belief, or just an outright arrogance of being more intelligent than any other living species on earth. These people just feel threatened by this dangerously wonderful idea and are not ready to accept the fact that all livings things have a common heritage. We share the same DNA with the same four bases; Thymine, Cytosine, Adenine and Guanine to convey the genetic information and the same twenty amino acid to form our proteins. We share sixty percent of our genes with a banana, ninety percent with mice, and 98.75%[13] with the chimpanzee our closest known relative. This is the beauty, that God devised such a wonderful system (of evolution) which has created an immense biodiversity on this planet Earth.

When a small seed is planted in the ground, it grows into a big tree with main stem, branches, twigs and leaves. Life originated in similar fashion out of organic and inorganic chemicals of the earth, and formed the first "stem cell" and then branched into every kind of life including the plant life here each twig represents one species. From the first stem cell, to traceable fossil record of life, took billions of years.

5

THE MECHANISM OF EVOLUTION

Human civilization is less than ten thousand years old. We took some plants and animals from the wild for our food and tried to improve their quality by artificially selecting the best. The plants and animals changed drastically due to these efforts. During the last two hundred years the improvement in the livestock and plants has reached to its peak due to increased scientific knowledge. Now we have created the supper cow (Holstein) which can produce 22,000 pounds of milk in one year, a supper chicken (Leghorn) which can lay 300 eggs a year. In the field of grains, fruits and vegetables we have the same success story. Take the case of dogs; starting with some wild species we have created dogs in huge range of shapes and sizes. These plants and animals never existed in the wild which we have created. What I am trying to say is that we human beings have managed to bring about these tremendous changes in a fraction of a second in terms of geological time. Think what can happen in millions of years in the crucible of nature?

It is a very common question people ask: why an organism did not change but its progeny evolved into a different species? This is a very good question; the answer is very simple; every creature on earth is a product of its environment, time and food it consumes. Take the case of the Yak: it has a body of a cow except it has long hairs on its body to protect it from the cold. The ancestors of the yak and cow are the same but one branch of the ancestors chose to live at high altitudes where it was cold and separated from rest of the herd, so they developed long hairs to protect them from cold and evolved into the yak. The same reasoning can be applied to all the animals and plants found in nature.

The mechanism of evolution has three simple steps. Mutation, variation and natural selection. Though it sounds very simple there is more to it than these three main steps. A new concept of epigenetic mark is being added to this three main steps which has been discussed in this chapter. The new concept is changing the mechanism of evolution giving a much better picture where the organism participates in its own evolutionary process.

Our basic thinking of gen-centered version of evolution is undergoing a change. What is emerging is a synthesis between gene-centered which has dominated for the last 55 years and new epigenetic mark concept. The new concept is, that evolutionary change can result from instruction as well as selection so some mutations are nonrandom.[14] Also there is more to heredity than just genes.

The Human body has trillions of cells and each cell has a nucleus which holds our 25,000 genes. The genes provide the code for producing proteins and other important functions. On the top of the genes we have various chemicals called epigenetic mark which offers basic instruction to genes telling them to switch on or off. Epigenetic mechanisms play important roles in our development from a fertilized egg into a complex human being, as well as in aging and in various diseases including cancer. Stressors like environment and rich diet can activate epigenetic marks by adding a methyl group to DNA and can be passed down to your offspring in one generation. If the environmental pressure is removed, the epigenetic marks will eventually fade. On the other hand if it is not removed the epigenetic marks may become permanent and lead the organism towards evolution by initiating the developmental changes. These developmental changes are non-arbitrary, being determined by the dynamics of the epigenetic system itself. Developmental changes may be assimilated into the new organism as a whole, which set the parameters for further evolution. Development and evolution can become a continuous process with the organism participating in shaping its own developmental and evolutionary history. Epigenetic marks explains why some species evolve so fast while others stay the same for millions of years. It explains how a small fish eating mammal evolved into a big fully marine mammal in relatively short geological time period of 13 million years and finally into a blue whale, the largest animal ever to live on earth in a matter of 35 more million years.

Mutation is defined as a change in the genetic material either in DNA or RNA. It can happen by copying errors in the genetic material during the cell division, by exposure to radiation by chemicals (mutagens), by change of environment and even by viruses. Mutation in the gene can be neutral, beneficial or harmful for the organisms. In a multicellular organism, mutation can be subdivided into germline mutations, which can be passed on to descendants and somatic mutation which cannot be transmitted. So mutation creates diverse gene pool and when the mutated organism becomes isolated geographically in a different environment than its parent organism it starts to adapt to the new environment. In the process of adaptation the offspring after several generations becomes quite different from the original individual and becomes a new species. In biological terms the accumulation of changes in the gene over time is called the genetic drift which is responsible for the creation of the new species. Darwin's finches in the Galapagos islands are an excellent example; how one species of finch evolved into several species simply because they have to adapt to a different condition in each island specially food. The same is true of the Hawaiian honeycreepers, a group of 23 species of birds ranging from four to eight inches. These birds are very closely related because they descend from a common ancestor. The ancestors of these birds found an open ecological niche in each island and quickly evolve the characteristics to exploit those niches.

Natural selection is one of the basic tools of evolution, along with the mutation, variation, isolation and epigenetic mark. Since the environment cannot support unlimited growth, not all individuals get to reproduce to their full potential. The organism which can adapt to the new environments will survive, in other words survival of the fittest in the struggle for existence happens because of limited resources. Whether you like it or not, that is how nature (God's plan) works. This is the reason why 99.9 % of the species which existed in the past became extinct today. That 0.1% which have survived are called living fossils because they virtually remained unchanged for hundreds of millions of years. Mass extinction is a rare event which happened sixty five million years ago during the Cretaceous period. Human activity of the last ten thousand years have increased extinction rate to an unprecedented scale matching those of Cretaceous period. Some experts have estimated that fifty percent of the existing species may become extinct by the end of the 21st century.

An example of evolution resulting from natural selection was discovered among "peppered" moths living near English industrial cities. These insects vary in wing and body coloration from light to dark. During the 19th century, sooty smoke from coal burning furnaces killed the lichen on trees and darkened the bark. When moths landed on these trees and other blackened surfaces, the dark colored ones were harder to spot by birds who ate them and subsequently, they more often lived long enough to reproduce. Over generations the environment continued to favor darker moths. As a result, they progressively became more common. By 1895, 98% of the moths in the vicinity of English cities like Manchester were mostly black. Since the 1950's, air pollution controls have significantly reduced the amount of heavy particulate air pollutants reaching the trees, buildings, and other objects in the environment. As a result, lichen has grown back, making trees lighter in color. Now, natural selection favors lighter moth varieties so they have become the most common. This trend has been well documented by field studies undertaken between 1959 and 1995 by Sir Cyril Clarke from the University of Liverpool.

No aspect of biomedical research seems more urgent today than the study of those microbial diseases. The capacity for quick change among disease-causing microbes is what makes them so dangerous. By natural selection they acquire resistance to drugs that should kill them. There is no better or immediate evidence supporting the theory of evolution than this process of forced transformation among our inimical germs. The cost of treating penicillin-resistant and methicillin-resistant staph infection costs 30 billion dollars a year in the United States alone. Recently a man infected with Tuberculosis made a trip from USA to Europe which made headlines all over the world. Why? Because he was infected with a drug resistant Tuberculosis bacterium which is the creation of mutation, variation and natural selection the simple mechanisms of evolution. If we do not understand the evolutionary forces at work, we human beings will pay a heavy price in the end. Muslims who refuse to understand the workings of universe and nature will probably pay a much higher price.

Evolution and Randomness

The creationists say that the basis of the Darwinian evolution lie on two basic assumptions: changes in morphologies are induced by random mutations on the genome, and natural selection. They argue that an organized life can't come from a random process and chance. But they don't understand that in nature, order from randomness are very common. Snowflakes, tornadoes, and lightning are just a few examples of order coming from randomness in nature. All this natural phenomenon require no intelligent program to achieve that order. Stephenson J Gould the famous Harvard evolutionist has written about the different senses of randomness and chance in science:

> In ordinary English, a random event is one without order, predictability or pattern. The word connotes disaggregation, falling apart, formless anarchy, and fear. Yet, ironically, the scientific sense of random conveys a precisely opposite set of associations. A phenomenon governed by chance yields maximal simplicity, order and predictability--at least in the long run. Thus, if you wish to understand patterns of long historical sequences, pray for randomness.

It is true that the vast majority of known mutations are unadaptive and random. But there are many mutation which are adaptive. The concept of epigenetic marks explains why some mutations are not random. When organism comes in contact with different environment and diet it can activate epigenetic marks which turns the gene on and off. Epigenetic marks may become permanent and lead the organism towards evolution by initiating the developmental changes. These developmental changes can initiate a nonrandom adaptive mutation. The evolution of elephant from a small pig like mammal is an excellent example. All the developmental change must have happened due to nonrandom adaptive mutation.

Randomness and Chance certainly play a big part in evolution, but don't ignore the fundamental role of natural selection, which is the very opposite of chance. Chance and randomness in the form of mutations, provides vast pool of genetic variation, which is the raw material for the natural selection. It sorts out certain variations, those variations which give greater reproductive success to their possessors are retained, and less successful variations are weeded out quickly. When the environment changes, or when organisms move to a different environment, different variations are selected, leading eventually to a different species. Harmful mutations usually die out so they don't interfere with the process of beneficial mutations. It is chance and randomness which have created an immense variety of life on planet Earth; otherwise our world would have turn into a very boring place.

6

ETCHED ON STONE

Evolution is really a story of logic extended backwards into time, if we take into account the natural history of the Earth. To reconstruct the story you have to have the evidence. The evidence in this case is the fossils record preserved in different layers of the earth literally etched on stone. The layers of the earth are like pages of the book written by nature (God), where the story of evolution is hidden, you have to decipher it.

Most of the rocks exposed at the surface of the Earth are sedimentary, formed from particles of older rocks that have been broken apart by water or wind. The gravel, sand, and mud settle to the bottom in rivers, lakes, and oceans. These sedimentary particles may bury living and dead animals and plants on the lake or sea bottom. With the passage of time and the accumulation of more particles, and often with chemical changes, the sediments at the bottom of the pile become rock. Gravel becomes a rock called conglomerate, sand becomes sandstone, mud becomes mudstone or shale, and the animal skeletons and plant pieces can become fossils.

Sedimentary rocks are formed particle by particle and bed by bed, and the layers are piled one on top of the other.

Thus, in any sequence of layered rocks, a given bed must be older than any bed on top of it. This Law of Superposition is fundamental to the interpretation of Earth history, because at any one location it indicates the relative ages of rock layers and the fossils in them. The figure 1 on page 28 shows how the fossils have been found in different layers of the Earth. The older layers have fossils of less advanced organism. As we study the layer above the lower level we find the fossils of advanced organism.

The story of life is indeed very old. How life on Earth could have arisen from inanimate matter is the subject of abiogenesis, it has nothing to do with evolution, which is the study of how groups of living things change over time. The first living things on Earth are thought to be single cell photosynthetic bacteria perhaps evolved from pool of organic chemicals. The oldest ancient fossil microbe-like objects are dated to be 3.5 billion years old approximately one billion years after the formation of the Earth itself. This simple bacteria ruled the Earth for two billion years, after which we find the trace of eukaryotes a bacteria with cell containing nuclei and chromosome.[15,16] Then, around 600 million years ago, a bunch of multicellular organism came into existence which included jellyfish, sponges and worms. By the Cambrian period, about 540 million years ago, we have a rapid divergent evolution of invertebrate, like trilobite, mollusks and brachiopods etc. The body structures of these creatures were well defined and a huge number of fossils can be found in the layer of the Cambrian period. Recently a small eel like chordate called *Haikouella lanceolata*[17] has been found in a layer 530 million years old located in China. Most likely this is the earliest chordate, the group which gave rise to all vertebrates. In this tiny creature lies the seed of evolution of all the vertebrates including human being.

By the end of Cambrian which is about 470 million years ago we find the fossil of primitive vertebrate, a creature with a back bone called chordates. These primitive vertebrates evolved into a jaw less fish by the end of the Ordovician period about 450 million years ago and finally into a full-fledged fish numerous in variety during the Silurian period (443-417 million years ago).

The Devonian period (417-354 million years ago) brought a great change on the land itself. We find the fossils of small plants, lots of ferns and seed producing plants. The land was ready to receive the guests from the sea. The fish were in transition to become tetrapods.[18] We find the first fossils of tetrapods (Four legged creature) a land living vertebrate during this period.

The Carboniferous period occurred from about 354- 290 million years ago, an age of tremendous vegetation growth, which was responsible for the formation of coal throughout the world. In addition to the formation of coal, one major biological event occurred which was the formation of an amniotic egg.[19] This was a big evolutionary step which allowed the ancestors of reptile, birds and mammals to fully exploit the virgin land.

The Permian period lasted from 290 to 248 million years ago and was the last period of the Paleozoic Era. This period is recognized for the largest mass extinction of marine invertebrates. On land, the fern like plants flourished[20] which paved the way for the age of dinosaurs. This is the period when the primitive forms of dinosaurs appeared.

The Triassic and Jurassic periods were the age of the dinosaurs which lasted well into the Cretaceous period (250 to 65 million years). All kinds of dinosaurs evolved during this period including the meat-eating giant

Tyrannosaurus rex, gigantic herbivore, Diplodocus and many others. Jurassic saw the origination of the first bird namely a well-known Archaeopteryx which had the characteristic of both birds and small dinosaurs. Small warm blooded mammals also appeared by the end of Jurassic[21]. Flowering plants and the first representatives of the modern tree appeared during the Cretaceous period. The super continent of Pangaea completed its breakup into present day continent during this period. By the end of Cretaceous which was the last period of Mesozoic era, when a huge number of species became extinct and the golden age of dinosaurs was about to end, this period is called the great age of dying on land.

The end of Cretaceous marked the extinction of all non-feathered dinosaurs and the beginnings of new forms of life. The Cenozoic era which covers 65 million years to present day, is the ongoing era. The Cenozoic is the age of new life. During this era, mammals diverged from a few small generalized forms into a diverse collection of terrestrial and marine animals. The Cenozoic era is the age of savannas, where flowering plants and insects evolved in symbiotic relationships. Some mammals went back to the sea, to exploit the new resources and evolved into one of the biggest animal ever lived on this planet: the blue whale. During this era the continents fully separated from each other, so the evolution of the plants and animals took a slightly different path and produced a variety different fauna and flora in each continent. Australia which was separated from the super continent before the establishment of placental mammal took its own evolutionary path and produced all marsupial animals, not found anywhere except for one or two small rodents like creature similar to the opossum.

The first very small primates called *prosimians* appeared

by the beginning of the Cenozoic era about 54 million years ago. The first monkey appeared some 34 million years ago and the first ape 23 million years ago.[22] Some of the great apes of Africa faced a process of an expanding savanna some six million years ago. To survive, these apes had to walk on two legs and so around five to six million years ago these apes perfected the bipedal locomotion. This event was the turning point in the history of evolution for mankind. The two hands became free and this great asset, finally transformed the great ape from animality to humanity and we as Muslims can state that's how God planned it.

These are not the stories from the book of Harry Potter but is the real geological history of the earth etched on stone deciphered by the scientists of the twentieth century. The natural history of the earth clearly demonstrates without any doubt that evolution has taken place and this is just one evidence out of many which point towards evolution.

7

THE PREDICTIVE POWER OF THE THEORY OF EVOLUTION

A central tenet in science is that a scientific theory is supposed to have predictive power, and verification of predictions are seen as an important and necessary support for the theory. Examples of predictive power of Dmitri Mendeleev's (Russian chemist) use of his periodic table to predict previously undiscovered chemical elements and their properties is very famous in science. His predictions proved to be correct and later on after his death the elements were discovered with properties as predicted. Another example of predictive power is the prediction of Einstein's General Theory of Relativity that the path of light would bend in the presence of a strong gravitational field. This was experimentally verified during the solar eclipse of 1919.

Darwin while presenting his Theory of Evolution predicted the presence of many transitional forms of fossils. Sure enough, thousands of such fossils have been found: like intermediate between fish and early tetrapods, between dinosaurs and birds, humans and great ape this can go on and on.

Humans are most closely related to the great apes that are indigenous to Africa . Why did the Leakeys, and others went to Africa in search of early hominid fossils? Why not dig in Australia, North America, South America. Darwin gave an answer for this question more than a century ago, long before any early hominid fossils had been found.

> "We are naturally led to inquire, where was the birthplace of man at that stage of descent when our progenitors diverged from the Catarrhine stock? The fact that they belonged to this stock clearly shows that they inhabited the Old World; but not Australia nor any oceanic island, as we may infer from the laws of geographical distribution. In each great region of the world the living mammals are closely related to the extinct species of the same region. It is therefore probable that Africa was formerly inhabited by extinct apes closely allied to the gorilla and chimpanzee; and as these two species are now man's nearest allies, it is somewhat more probable that our early progenitors lived on the African continent than elsewhere."[23]

Thus, the theory of evolution predicts that we may find early hominid fossils on the African continent. Numerous transitional fossils between humans and the great apes have been found in southern and eastern Africa. These examples include such fossil species as *Australopithecus anamensis, Australopithecus afarensis, Australopithecus garhi, Kenyanthropus platyops, Kenyanthropus rudolfensis, Homo habilis*, and most recently *Ardipithecus ramidus.* A host of other transitional fossils not related to *Homo sapiens*, such as the *robust australopithicenes* have also been found on the African continent.

Paleontologists had found fossils of amphibians with necks, and four legs, in rock 365 million years old. On the other hand rocks more than 385 million years old had only fish fossils, with no amphibian characteristics. The theory of evolution predicted that since amphibians evolved from fish, an intermediate form should be found in rock between 385 to 365 million years old . Such an intermediate form should have many fish like characteristics, like scales but also should have many amphibian characteristics as well. Dr. Neil Shubin of the University of Chicago made an expedition to islands in the Canadian arctic searching specifically for this fossil form rocks that were 375 million years old. After four years of frustration and hard work in arctic cold, he discovered the fossils in 2004. In honor of local Inuit people the fossil was named Tiktaalik ("Tiktaalik" means large fresh water fish in Inuit). This fossil has the characteristic of fish, like scales, gills and more robust fins and at the same time has amphibian features. It has a flat head with eyes and nostrils on the top of the skull and a neck a feature absent in fish. Tiktaalik with its robust fin was well adapted to crawl about and peek above the surface of water to breath air. In the fish's fins, the scientists found evidence of limbs in the making. There are the beginnings of digits, proto-wrists, elbows and shoulders. The fish also had a flat skull resembling a crocodile's, a neck, ribs and other parts that were similar to four--legged land animals known as tetrapods.

This marvelous fossil connects fish with tetrapods so wonderfully and at the same time highlights the predictive power of the theory of evolution. DR. Neil Shubin announced his find in April, 2006 which made headlines all over the world.[24] He writes about it in his book: *Your Inner Fish.*

> Though for me the greatest moment of the whole media blitz was not seeing the political cartoons or reading the editorial coverage and the heated discussion on the blog. It took place at my son's preschool. In the midst of the press hubbub, my son's preschool teacher asked me to bring in the fossil and describe it. I dutifully brought a cast of Tiktaalik into Nathaniel's class, bracing myself for the chaos that would ensue. The twenty, four- and five-year-olds were surprisingly well behaved as I described how we have worked in the Arctic to find the fossil and showed the animal's sharp teeth. Then I asked what they thought it was. Hands shot up. The first child

> said it was a crocodile or lizard it has a flat head with eyes on the top. Big teeth, too. Other children started to voice their dissent: No, no it isn't a crocodile; it is a fish, because it has scales and fin. Yet another child shouted, "Maybe it is both" Tiktaalik's message is so straightforward even preschoolers can see it.

Mr. Harun Yahya should make a trip to Chicago and meet those preschoolers and learn some lessons from them and pay six million dollars to Dr. Neil Shubin, the prize he has set for someone who could find a transitional fossil.[25] If he still does not believe that Tiktaalik is an intermediate fossil between fish and tetrapods then he must be looking for the fossil of "Fronkey" with body of a frog and a head of a monkey or an "Elephanzee" a body of an elephant and head of a chimpanzee. If those kinds of fossils are found, then definitely the theory of evolution is doomed.

Because of similarity between birds and *theropods* a small dinosaurs that walked on two legs led paleontologists to theorize that bird evolved from theropods. Fossil record of 200 million year old rocks shows plenty of theropods but no bird like features. Around 70 million years ago we find, fossils of birds which look fairly modern. If evolution is true we should find fossils of reptile-bird transitions in rocks between 70 to 200 million years old.

A few years after the publication of Charles Darwin's *The Origin of Species*, British biologist Thomas Henry Huxley, who was a supporter of the theory of evolution, proposed that birds were descendants of dinosaurs. He compared the skeletal structure of a small theropod dinosaurs, and the first bird Archaeopteryx found in rock 14millioyearsold.In 1868 he published an article on the animals which are most nearly intermediate between birds and reptiles.

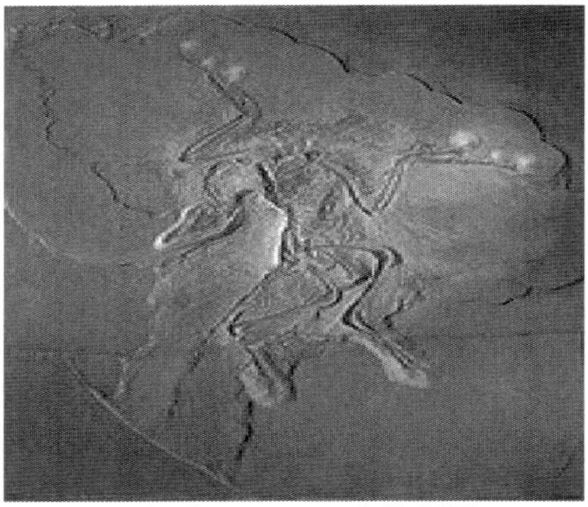
Archaeopteryx 142 MYA

Compsognathus 153 MYA

Coelophysis 225 MYA

After a century of evolutionary prediction without conclusive evidence for a while, a well preserved fossils of feathered dinosaurs have been discovered during the 1990s in China and more continue to be found every year. A total of 24 such transitional fossils have been found as predicted by the theory of evolution in the rocks between 200 to 70 million years old. All these fossils have long tails and teeth like dinosaurs and wings and feathers like a birds. The fossils were preserved in a Lagerstatte, a sedimentary deposit in Liaoning, China exhibiting remarkable richness and completeness.

Not too long ago there was a large gap in the fossil record of the cetaceans (Whales, Dolphins). A recent discoveries from India and Pakistan has filled this gap. Theory of evolution predicted fossil of primitive whales should have hind legs even if they were fully aquatic. Sure enough we found the fossil of *Dorudon* a fully marine whale 16 feet long with two vestigial hind legs. Similarly the fossil of *Aetiocetus* shows the presence both teeth and beeline as predicted by the theory of evolution.

Humans and other primates do not have the capability to make Vitamin C. The theory of evolution predicts the ancestors of humans should have this function as do most other animals. So it is natural we expect that humans, other primates should carry evidence of this lost function on molecular level. Nishikimi[26] and others made the prediction and sure enough the gene required for Vitamin C synthesis was found in humans and other primates. It is present as a pseudogene, incapable of functioning. Vitamin C pseudogene has been found in other primates, exactly as predicted by evolutionary theory. The DNA sequences for this broken gene in chimpanzees, orangutans, and macaques have also been done. As predicted, the human and chimpanzee pseudogenes are the most similar, followed by the human and orangutan genes, followed by the human and macaque genes, exactly as predicted by the evolutionary theory. Not only this, all of these genes have accumulated mutations at the exact rate predicted.

Insect wings evolved from gills, with an intermediate stage of skimming on the water surface. Since the primitive surface-skimming condition is widespread among stoneflies, J. H. Marden predicted that stoneflies would likely retain other primitive traits, too. This prediction led to the discovery in stoneflies a functional hemocyanin, used for oxygen transport in other arthropods but never before found in insects.[27] Ernst Mayr a 20th century leading evolutionary biologist of Harvard university predicted in 1954 that speciation should be accompanied with faster genetic evolution. A phylogenetic analysis of the species have supported his prediction which is based on the theory of evolution.

The earliest marsupial fossils have been discovered in the rocks of Cretaceous period, when South America, Antarctica, and Australia were still connected. The theory evolution predicts that extinct marsupials fossil should be found in South America and Antarctica, since marsupials must have traversed these continents to reach their present day location in Australia. Sure enough we have found lots of marsupial fossils both on South America and Antarctica. This is an astounding confirmation of the predictive power the theory of evolution, given that no marsupials live on Antarctica now.

Can the creationists explain why only the continent of Australia has marsupials? They can't. But the theory of evolution and the theory of continental drift can. The marsupials were present in every continents. During the evolutionary process they just could not compete with the more advanced placental mammals so they died out. The continent of Australia separated from the supercontinent of *Gondwanaland* before the establishment of placental mammals. Australia being a small continent the marsupials who came from the supercontinent through Antarctica had no competition with the advanced mammals, so the evolution took its own unique course and created only marsupials.

8

TRANSITIONAL FOSSILS

Transitional fossils are one of the main evidence which proves the theory of evolution beyond doubt because the theory predicts those kinds of fossils. When something dies, it is usually eaten by other creatures, disassembled, and digested; especially smaller animals. Rarely is anything ever fossilized, and even fewer things are very well-preserved. The conditions required for that process of fossilization are very particular and special. Therefore the fossil record can only represent a very small fraction of everything that has ever lived. But despite of this, a huge number of fossils which we call intermediate or transitional have been discovered and new ones are added every year. But creationists still insist that we've never found a single one, because what they usually ask us to present are impossible like "Crocoduck" with a head of a crocodile and a body of a duck which evolution will never allow to happen.

About 530 million years ago we find the fossil of a very tiny chordate about an inch long. With the passage of geological time this tiny chordate evolved into bigger ones and then to jaw less fish with back bones and finally to normal fish and all the transitional fossils have been found.

Hynerpeton 360 MYA

Acanthostega gunnari 365 MYA

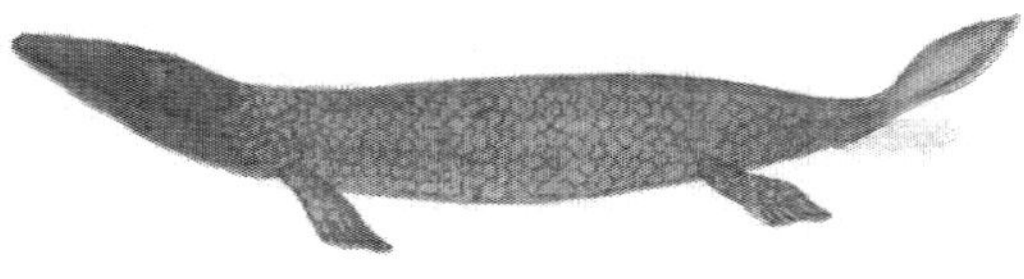

Tiktaalik roseae 375 MYA

Eusthenopteron foordi 385 MYA

Evolution tetrapods from fish

About 390 million years ago fishes were the only vertebrates on the planet Earth. Some of them evolved into lobe finned fish like *Eusthenopteron foordi* by 385 million years ago. This fish had large bony fins which allowed it to walk on mud. This fish had both gills and lungs. Ten million years later we find a transitional creature *Tiktaalik roseae* which I have discussed in great detail. Then by 365 million years ago we find the fossil of first tetrapod *Acanthostega gunnari* with eight limb bones. And finally five million years later a true tetrapods; *Hynerpeton* with five limb bones. The structure of the shoulder girdle indicates this animal may have been one of the earlier, more primitive tetrapods to evolve during the Devonian. It evolved complex lungs to exploit the oxygen rich atmosphere.

The transitional fossil Tiktaalik, confirms elements of a major transition in evolution between fishes and tetrapods. Similarly the Archaeopteryx found in rock 142 million old years reminds us the transition between dinosaurs and birds. These facts are a powerful rebuttal to religious creationists, who have long argued that the absence of such transitional creatures is a serious weakness in Darwin's theory of evolution.

Evolution of Elephant

Elephants are the sole living members of an order of mammals known as *Proboscidea*, which includes elephants and mammoths. Many transitional fossils of Elephant have been found in Africa and other parts of the world. Here is the history of the evolution of an elephant derived from transitional fossils.

Moeritherium was a pig-like animal, about 35 inches high, and resembling the tapirs is regarded as the ancestor of the elephant family which lived about 50 million years ago. *Moeritherium* was probably semi-aquatic, living in rivers and lakes mainly feeding on water plants. The eyes and ears were placed high on the head, always above the surface when swimming, it had no trunk, but its nose was long like a tapirs.[28]

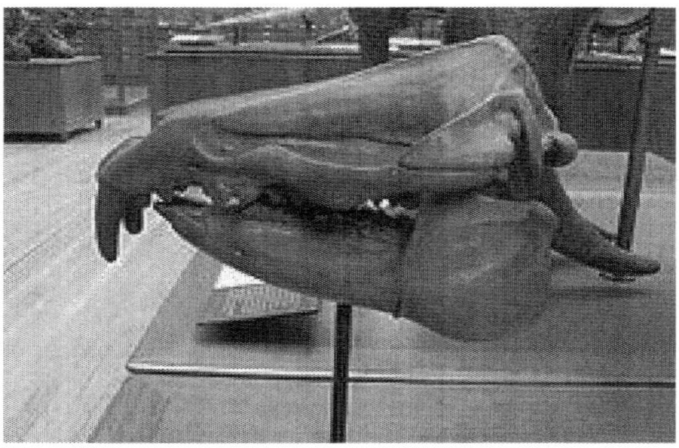

FIGURE 2. Fossil of *Moeritherium*

FIGURE 3.Fossil of *Gomphotherium*

Palaeomastodon is believed to have been more closely related to *Moeritherium*, the earliest proboscid. This early elephant lived about 35 million years ago. It is distinguished by its scoop-shaped lower tusks, which it used to dredge plants from flooded river and lake.

Gomphotherium is regarded as the ancestor to mammoths and both the present living species of elephants which lived about 24 million years ago. *Gomphotherium* had both upper and lower incisors the skull was elongate and low and they were probably adapted for a life in lakes and swamps.[29]

Primelephas is regarded as the first elephant which lived some six million years ago. It is important to note here that it was the immediate ancestor of both modern elephants and the woolly mammoth. It had large size tooth structure and a long trunk with four tusks two upper and two lower. The lower tusks were shorter than the upper tusks. *Primelephas* was close to the modern elephants. Here we see how a small pig like animal evolved into elephant in 50 million years which has been illustrated on page 57.

Modern Elephant

Primelephas 6MYA

Gomphotherium 24 MYA

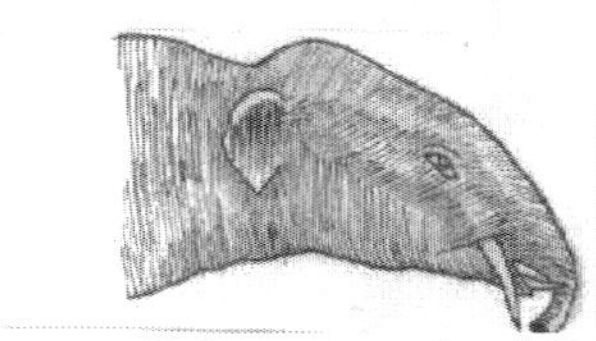

Palaeomastodon 34MYA

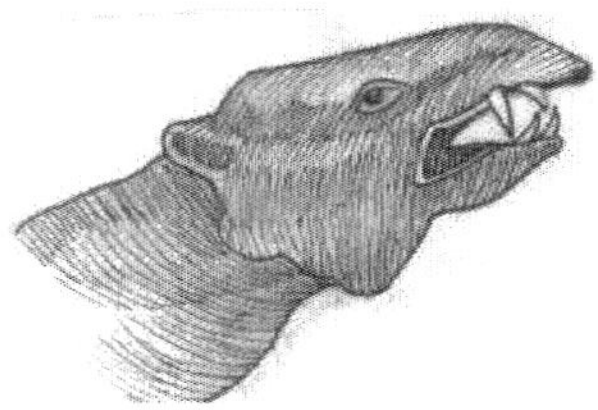

Moeritherium 50 MYA

Evolution of Whale

About 45 to 55 million years ago, the ocean was very rich with life like fish and other creatures in shallow water. Mammals were diversifying on land, and there was a lot of competition for food. So, some mammals began living part of their lives in the ocean to feed them self. After some time they began living all of their lives in the ocean. Philip Gingerich, a University of Michigan paleontologist and his team have discovered the transitional fossils of the land mammal to whales in Pakistan and other places. Here is the history of evolution of whale according to transitional fossils.

The ancestors of whales; *Ambulocetus,* looked rather like a huge otter with fur. It had a long low body with short powerful limbs. Its back legs in particular seemed to be used for propulsion, and its feet had long webbed toes. Its tail was slightly flattened, like that of an otter, to help it swim. Its eyes and nostrils were on the top of its skull, allowing it to see and breathe whilst partly submerged in water, and it had a fearsome set of teeth. *Ambulocetus* lived 50-49 million years ago. It descended from a land-living carnivorous animal a big dog like creature called *Pakicetus.* This animal lived some 53 million years ago and started eating fish from shallow water of the sea.[30] Both fossils have been discovered in Pakistan.

Rodhocetus a larger, more streamlined mammal spent most of its time in the water which lived around 47 million years ago. Its splay-footed posture shows that it was capable of rather dragging itself on land. As further evidence of the increasingly aquatic lifestyle of early whales, the hip bones of *Rodhocetus* weren't fused to its backbone, which gave it improved flexibility when swimming in the water.

Dorudon was a fully aquatic mammal with a short neck and blow holes on the top of its head which lived around 40 million years ago. They could not have come back on land to spend any time because their pelvis and hind limbs were greatly reduced compared to their size (16 feet). It seems that hind limbs were present as a vestigial organ. Closely related to *Basilosaurus*, *Dorudon* were shorter and more compact. When they were first found, in the same deposits as *Basilosaurus*, the two animals were so similar that at first *Dorudon* were thought to be baby *Basilosaurus*. They are, in fact, different species and now the fossils of baby *Dorudon* have also been found. [31]

Aetiocetus is described as having both teeth and baleens. Its skull features indicates it was a primitive mysticeti, the group that contain all the baleen whales. This whale lived some 25 million years ago. The origin of baleen and the loss of teeth are correlated with the evolution of obligate filter-feeding in mysticeti whales. The transitional fossils between tooth bearing and fully baleen whale are so interesting. This whale must be hunting big fish and supplementing its diet with small creature like krill. With an abundance of krill the big whale lost its teeth and evolved into a baleen whale.

It is remarkable that evolutionary force changed a small land mammal to *Aetiocetus* a fully marine mammal of about 25 feet long in a short geological time of 25 million years. With the change of climate and availability of new food (Krill) it took another 20 million years to evolve into modern whales, specially the blue whale with baleen plate in place of teeth. Blue whales are the largest animals ever known to have lived on Earth. These magnificent marine mammals grow up to 100 feet long and weighing upwards to 200 tons. Blue whales reach these mind-boggling dimensions on a diet composed exclusively of tiny shrimp like creature called krill. With the availability of abundant krill evolution created a mouth which could harvest 4 tons of krill a day, designed a heart equal to size of small car and a body which could give birth to a 3 ton and 25 feet long baby and provide milk for the calf to gain 200 Lb a day. No doubt evolution has created the greatest show on earth as said by Richard Dawkins.

This series of transitional fossils of whales depicted on page 61 is a powerful argument for evolution. The timing of the fossils is right, and the progression of fossils towards becoming a whale is evident. A big fully marine mammal *Dorudon* has vestigial hind legs which proves without doubt that it has evolved from a land mammal. It would be hard to imagine asking for better evidence than the evolution of a whale.

FIGURE 4. Skeleton of a blue whale

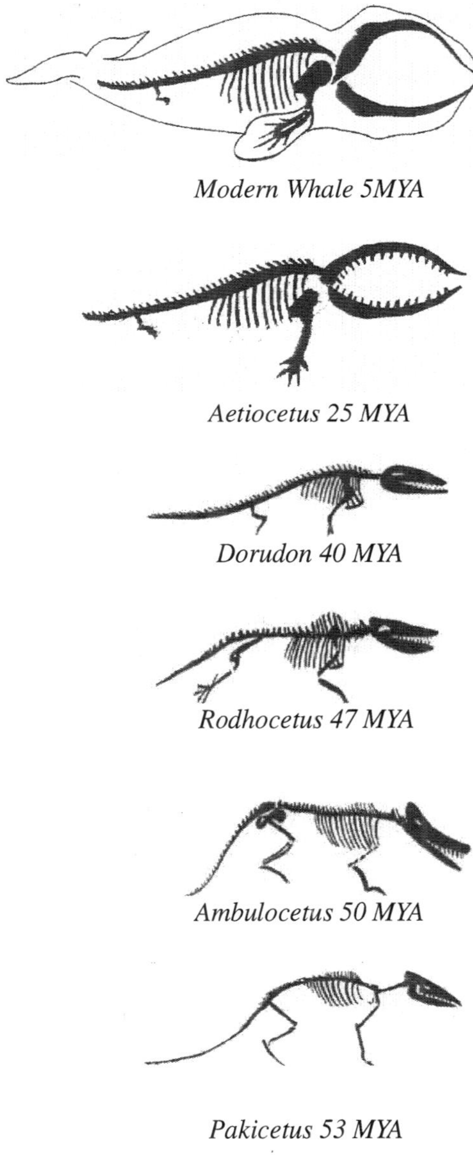

FIGURE 5 *Shows the gradual transformation from land to marine mammal*

9

VESTIGE AND ATAVISM

Some of the most renowned evidence for evolution are the various nonfunctional organs found both in anatomical and a molecular level in humans and other creatures. A vestige is defined, independently of evolutionary theory, as a reduced and rudimentary structure compared to the same complex structure in other organisms. Vestigial characters, if functional, perform relatively simple functions using structures that were clearly designed for more complex function. Many vestigial organs have no functions or have minor use.

The appendix is a vestige of the cesium, an organ to digest cellulose by human's herbivorous ancestors. Analogous organs in other animals similar to humans continue to perform that function, whereas other meat-eating animals have similarly diminished appendices. In line with the possibility of vestigial organs developing new functions, some research suggests that the appendix may guard against the loss of symbiotic bacteria that help in digestion. It might have some minor use but its presence is a liability for the human race because if it gets infected resulting in death if not removed on time. Six percent of people have a chance to get an appendix infection in his or her life time which is a big number.

Another human vestigial structure is the coccyx, the four fused caudal vertebrae found at the base of the spine, exactly where most mammals and many other primates have external tails protruding from the back. Humans and other apes are some of the only vertebrates that lack an external tail as an adult. The coccyx is a developmental remnant of the embryonic tail that forms in humans and then is degraded and eaten by our immune system. Our internal tail is unnecessary for sitting or walking.[32]

Our ancestors, like other mammals, had a more acute sense of smell than we do now; humans have less than 98 odorant receptor OR genes, of which 70 percent are pseudogenes which is nonfunctional. We still carry those genes as other vestiges. Many other mammals, such as mice, cats and dogs have many of the same OR genes as us, but all of theirs genes are working. This is the reason their smelling power is so high compared to humans. The external ear muscles for movement of ears are present in humans too, but have no function, whereas many mammals use those muscles to move the external ear. Our canine teeth and now the third molars are the vestigial residue of our past ancestors.

An extreme case are the dolphins, which are the descendant of land mammals. It no longer has any need to smell volatile substance yet it has all OR genes, of which none are functional. This clearly proves that dolphin evolved from a land mammal and all the pseudogenes are vestige on a molecular level.

Atavism

Atavism is the reappearance of a lost character specific to a remote evolutionary ancestors. It is not observed in the parents or recent ancestors of the organism and is an extreme rarity in a population .

Probably the most well known case of atavism is found in the whales. Whales are known to be the descendants of terrestrial mammals that had hind limbs. Thus, we expect the possibility that rare mutant whales might occasionally develop atavistic hind limbs. In fact, there are many cases where whales have been found with rudimentary atavistic hind limbs in the wild.[33]

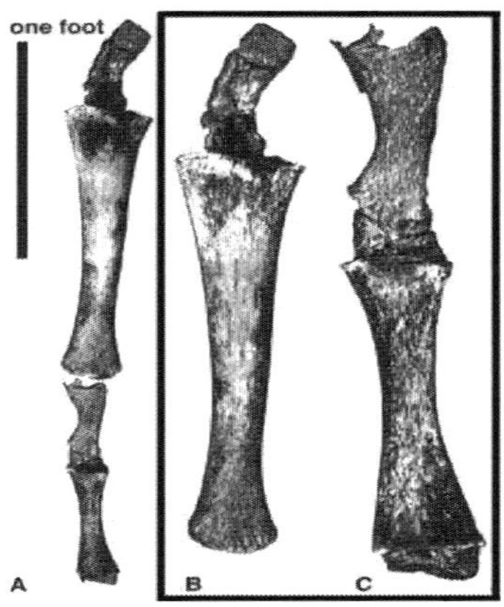

FIGURE 6.Atavistic hind-limb of a humpback whale

(Image taken from Andrew's article 1921)

Dolphins, along with whales and porpoises, are descendants of terrestrial mammals. The ancestors of the modern day dolphins entered the water roughly fifty million years ago. Modern dolphin skeletons have two small, rod-shaped pelvic bones thought to be vestigial hind limbs. In October 2006, an unusual bottlenose dolphin was captured in Japan; it had fins on each side of its genital slit which scientists believe to be a more pronounced development of these atavistic hind limbs. These limbs shows the evidence of the dolphin's four-limbed ancestry, as predicted from the common ancestry of dolphins and other land-dwelling mammals.

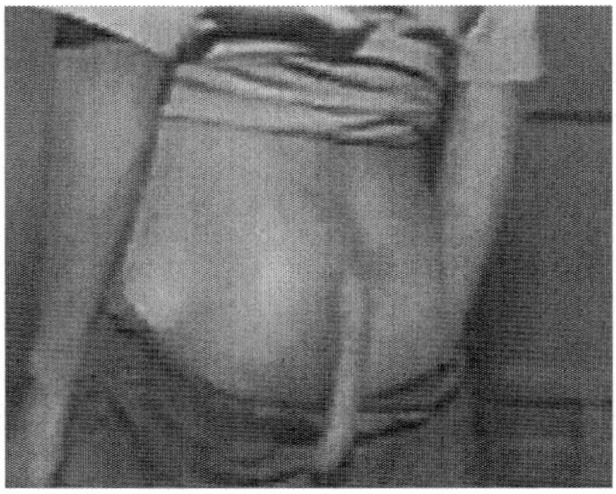

FIGURE 7. Human tail

Tails on humans are the exceptions that prove the evolutionary rule. Atavistic tail is possible, because genes for primitive traits haven't disappeared from our genome; they simply have been switched off. In rare cases, they are switched back on, allowing the so-called reverse evolution to takes place. If it happens, a child is born with human tail. This human atavisms reflects our common genetic heritage with other primate with tail. More than a 100 cases of human tails have been reported in medical literature. Most of the time it is surgically removed but in India people with tails are respected, because a Hindu God *Hanuman* himself had a big tail.

10

EMBRYOLOGY

Embryology and developmental biology have provided some excellent insights into evolutionary pathways. Morphological classifications of species are generally based on derived characters of adult organisms; embryology and developmental biology provide a nearly independent body of evolutionary evidence. The final adult structure of an organism is the product of numerous cumulative developmental processes. For a species to evolve morphologically, these developmental processes necessarily must have changed. But there are numerous examples in which an organism's evolutionary history is represented temporarily in its development stages.

Early in development, mammalian embryos temporarily have pharyngeal pouches, which are morphologically indistinguishable from aquatic vertebrate gill pouches like shark. This evolutionary relic reflects the fact that mammalian ancestors were once aquatic gill-breathing vertebrates. The pharyngeal pouches of modern fish embryos eventually become perforated to form gills. Mammalian pharyngeal pouches of course do not develop into gills, but rather give rise to structures that evolved from gills, such as the middle ears and tonsils etc.[34]

Hans Larsson of McGill University discovered that a four day old chick embryo's tail actually resembles the 16-

vertebrae similar to the reptiles, than the four to five vertebrae present in the developing spine of the chicken. As the embryo grew, the tail shortened until it contained the typical 5 vertebrae of the adult chicken. Matt Harris and John Fallon at the University of Wisconsin, noticed something strange in a 14 day old chicken embryonic head. Dissecting the beak, Harris and Fallon found saber-shaped structures identical to embryonic alligator teeth. These experiments clearly show that the genes of the dinosaurs are still present in chicken and turns on for a moment during early development stage. The new chicken gene takes care of the problem by releasing enzyme to dissolve the tail and the teeth and the chicks are born without big tails and teeth. But those days are not very far when biologist will create the chicks with long tails and teeth by reverse evolution by manipulating the genes of the chicken.

Like the chicken many species of snakes and legless lizards initially develop limb buds in their embryonic development, only to reabsorb them before birth. Similarly, modern adult dolphins, and porpoises have no hind legs. But still hind legs, complete with various developing leg bones, nerves, and blood vessels, temporarily appear in the fetus and then degenerate before birth. These facts are saying that these entire legless creatures have evolved from the ancestors with legs.

11

THE MOLECULAR BASIS OF EVOLUTION

When Charles Darwin proposed the Theory of Evolution, he almost did so in total ignorance of the disciplines we now know as genetics, cell biology, molecular biology, biochemistry, and paleontology. These branches of science have now gathered enormous amount of data that clearly support the theory of evolution. No scientific theory has been tested so thoroughly as the theory of evolution. The more detailed study of the living cell we do, the more we appreciate this theory. We have reached to the point beyond stones and bones where you no longer have to go into the field to look for fossils to solve many of the evolutionary puzzles, now it is being done inside a modern laboratory which was not possible only thirty years ago. Using the latest genetic technology, you can even see the evolution happening right before your eyes in a laboratory setting.

All living things have chromosomes in each cell, which have a component parts called gene. Genes are made of DNA which has all the information that creates the outward appearance of all living things as well as all the chemical processes that take place within them. Since we descended from a common ancestor we share a large percentage of genes which is common with all the living beings. The closely related living things will have a much higher percentage of similarity in their genetic constitution than the distantly related organisms in the evolutionary tree. This is the reason why the genes of chimpanzee and human beings have 98.77 % similarity while we share 90 % with a mouse and 89 % with a horse.

Phylogenetics is the science of estimating and analyzing evolutionary relationships. Molecular biology often helps in determining genetic relationships between different organisms. Nucleic acids (DNA and RNA) and proteins are *'information molecules'* in that they retain a record of an organism's evolutionary history. The approach is to compare nucleic acid sequences from different organisms using computer programs and estimate the evolutionary relationships based on the degree of homology between the sequences. Nucleic acids and proteins are linear molecules made of smaller units called nucleotides and amino acids, respectively. The nucleotide or amino acid differences within a gene reflect the evolutionary distance between two organisms. In other words, closely related organisms will exhibit fewer sequence differences than distantly related organisms.

One advantage of the molecular approach in determining phylogenetic relationships over the more classical approaches, such as those based on morphology or life cycle traits, is that the differences are readily quantifiable. Sequences from different organisms have been compared and the evolutionary relationship between the species have been established. The relationships between the species are exactly the same as determined by other methods and as predicted by the theory of evolution.

The cytochrome c is a class of proteins which serve in aerobic respiration. They are present in all aerobic organisms, including aerobic bacteria and humans. The molecular structure and the amino acid sequence vary between various species which makes it useful in the study of evolutionary divergence. A detail study has been done on the cytochrome c proteins of various organisms and the result has been compared with human cytochrome c protein. It is not surprising that both humans and chimpanzees have 100% identical molecule[35] (amino acid to amino acid) while 91.3% with a mouse, 88.5 % with a horse and 47.5 % with a *tetrahymena* (Ciliate protozoa). The molecular sequence evidence gives the most impressive and irrefutable evidence for the theory of evolution.

Blood is blood, it all looks alike, whether it is coming from a cow, goat, fish, chimp or human they all look red and performs the same functions in each species. If we inject a small amount of human blood plasma to a goat, the goat will develop the antibody to human blood proteins in a few weeks because the goat's immune system considers it as foreign protein quite different from his own. The blood plasma of the goat which has the antibody of human blood proteins when mixed with human blood plasma will form a white precipitate and the mixture will become quite turbid. The turbidity will increase as we do this experiment with evolutionary distant species, but the reverse is true if the species are closely related. Though we can't transfuse the chimpanzee's blood to humans, but when a small amount of blood plasma is injected to each other none of them develop the antibody to the blood proteins because the chimp or human immune system does not recognize it as a foreign protein; it is that close. Blood plasma turbidity test is another way of measuring the evolutionary closeness or distance between the species.

It has been observed that mutation in genes takes place at a regular rate thus the gene of the newly evolved species becomes a *gene clock* from which scientists use the rate to calibrate it. By analyzing the DNA of human and chimps and other species, even lice, scientists are finding out when and how speech developed, when our ancestors left Africa and when the two species diverged. Now DNA is getting the same importance as the fossils.

The researchers at Max Planck Institute for Evolutionary Anthropology in Germany have done the studies on the DNA of head lice and body lice. Head lice, as a species, go back millions of years, while body lice are a more recent arrival when our human ancestors must have lost their body hair for good – and started wearing fur or clothing to keep warm. Since new kinds of creatures tend to appear when a new habitat does, that's when head lice evolved into body lice. The fork in the louse's family tree occurred some 114,000 year ago according to the researchers of the Institute, and most probably that's when the human ancestors lost their body hair.

DNA hybridization can measure the similarity of DNA of different species. When strands of DNA are heated, they will separate at certain temperature and as they cool bond back together again. The temperature at which strands are separated is called the melting point. To compare different species, scientists cut the DNA of the species into small segments, separate the strands, and mix the DNA together. When the two specie's of DNA bonds together, the match between the two strands will not be perfect because of the genetic differences between the species. These weak bonds can be broken with just a little less heat, while closer matches require more heat to separate the strands again. The closer the species the higher the melting point and farther the species are lower is the melting point. In other words higher melting point is directly proportional to the closeness of the genes. Human, chimp, gorilla and orangutan genes when tested with this method the result came exactly as predicted by the theory of evolution. Chimps are closer to humans then gorilla followed by orangutan in the same order we have discovered this relationship by several other methods.[36]

Creationists ask the question; can you see the evolution happening in the laboratory? The answer is yes. With advanced genetic technology many complex biochemical pathways has been explained and observed in the laboratory using the evolutionary process of mutation and natural selection. The days are here now when every aspect of the evolutionary process of life can be understood and explained on molecular level. The evolution of bacteria has been observed in laboratory.

Bacteria grow very fast and in a matter of days it can have many generations. Twenty years ago, evolutionary biologist Richard Lenski of Michigan State University took a single Escherichia coli bacterium and used its descendants to find out how it evolves. After more than 44,000 generations, Lenski watched what happened. All bacteria evolved larger cells, for example, as well as faster growth rates on the glucose they were fed. Sometime around the 31,500th generation, something dramatic happened in just one of the populations - the bacteria suddenly acquired the ability to metabolize citrate, a second nutrient in their culture medium that E. coli normally cannot use. As a matter of fact the inability to use citrate is one of the traits by which bacteriologists distinguish E. coli from other species. The citrate-using mutants increased in population size and diversity. It is the most profound change which has been observed in this experiment. It also proves beyond a doubt that evolution can be experienced in laboratory setting.
Nylon is a synthetic fiber introduced in 1935. For a long

time bacteria could not consume it because they did not had proper enzyme to digest it. In 1975 a team of Japanese scientists[37] discovered a strain of bacteria living in ponds containing waste water from a factory producing nylon that was capable of digesting nylon even though those substances are not known to have existed prior to the invention of nylon. This new strain of bacteria produces an enzyme *nylonase* which break downs Nylon into small units so that it can be consumed as food. Scientists have repeated the Nylon eating experiment in a laboratory with another strain of bacteria and have succeeded. This clearly show that evolution can be observed as it occurs in laboratory setting.

There are many biochemical pathways involving evolution and has been observed in the laboratory setting but it is too technical to mention here in this book.

12

HUMAN EVOLUTION

The fact learned from the fossil records and recent advancement in genetics and molecular biology conforms that we humans have also evolved. It will be useless to go back and start our evolutionary path from the very first life in this chapter. Here I would like to discuss something about the first hominid who diverged from chimpanzee and became bipedal and his later generations.

The analysis of our gene and its molecular clock suggest that human-chimpanzee branched off some 5 to 6 million years ago. The same analysis estimate of 6.2 to 8.4 million years for the gorilla speciation suggesting that the gorilla lineage branched off 1.6 to 2.2 million years earlier than did the human-chimpanzee divergence. The most recent hominid fossil of Ardi is 4.4 million years old which fits very well with molecular clock analysis date. This hominid used to walk upright but its feet were still very close to a chimpanzee. It seems to be a transitional fossil between chimpanzee and Lucy a fully bipedal hominid 3.5 million years old. A chance of finding another fossil older than Ardi is slim but theoretically possible.

The *Ardipithecus ramidus (Ardi)* fossils were discovered in

Ethiopia's harsh Afar desert from where Lucy's species, *Australopithecus afarensis,* was found in 1974. Radiometric dating suggests that Ardi lived 4.4 million years ago and was 4 to 5 feet tall. All previously known hominids of our ancestral lineage walked upright on two legs, like us. But Ardi's feet, pelvis, legs, and hands suggest she was a biped on the ground but a quadruped when moving about on the trees. Her big toe, for instance, splays out from her foot like an ape, to get better grasp on tree limbs. Combined with modifications to the other toes, the bone would have helped Ardi walk upright on the ground, though less efficiently than later hominids like Lucy. It took 15 years and 47 scientists from 20 different countries to fully analyze the fossil of Ardi. [38]

Australopithecus afarensis (Lucy) lived between 3.9 and 3.0 million years ago. Its fossil was discovered by Don Johanson in 1974 in Afar region of Ethiopia. From this site 13 individuals were also uncovered and all were adults, with no injuries caused by carnivores. All 13 individuals seemed to have died at the same time, thus Don Johanson concluded that they might have been killed instantly from a flash flood. [39]

Lucy retained the apelike face with a sloping forehead, a distinct ridge over the eyes, a flat nose and a chinless lower jaw. It had a brain capacity of about 450 cc. It was between 3'6" and 5' tall. It was fully bipedal and the thickness of its bones showed that it was quite strong. Its weight to height ratio was about the same as the modern human but its head and face were proportionately much larger. This larger head with powerful jaws is a feature of all species prior to us.

Australopithecus africanus was quite similar to *afarensis* (Lucy) and lived between 3 and 2 million years ago. Its fossil were discovered in 1924 and more recently in 1992 all in South Africa. It was also bipedal, but was slightly larger in body size. Its brain size was also slightly larger, ranging up to 500 cc. The brain was not advanced enough for speech. The molars were a little larger than in *afarensis* and much smaller than modern human. This hominid was a herbivore and ate tough, hard to chew, plants. The shape of the jaw was now like the human.

Homo habilis was called the *handy man* because tools were found with his fossil remains. Its fossil was discovered by Mary and Louis Leakey in 1964 in Tanzania, Africa. This species existed between 2.4 and 1.5 million years ago. The brain size in earlier fossil specimens was about 500cc but rose to 800cc toward the end of the species life period. The species brain shape shows evidence that some speech had developed. *Habilis* was about 5' tall and weighed about 100 pounds.[40] Some scientists believe that *Habilis* is not a separate species and should be carried either as a later *Australopithecine* or an early *Homo erectus*.

Homo erectus lived between 1.8 million and 60,000 years ago. Its fossil have been found all over Asia[41] and Africa. Fossilized remains 1.8 and 1 million years old have been found in Indonesia, Georgia, Spain and Vietnam. It was a successful species for a million and a half years. Older fossils had a 900cc brain size on the average. The brain grew steadily during its reign. Toward the end its brain was almost the same size as modern man, at about 1200cc. The species definitely had speech. *Homo erectus* developed tools, weapons and fire and learned to cook his food. He traveled out of Africa into China and Southeast Asia and developed clothing for northern climates. He turned to hunting for his food. Only his head and face differed from modern man. Like *Homo habilis*, the face had massive jaws with huge molars, no chin, thick brow ridges, and a long low skull. He was sturdier in build and much stronger than the modern human.[42]

Homo sapiens (archaic) provides the bridge between *Homo erectus* and *Homo sapiens sapiens* (Modern man) during the period of 200,000 to 500,000 years ago. Many skulls have been found with features intermediate between the two. Brain averaged about 1200cc and speech was indicated. Skulls are more rounded and with smaller features. Molars and brow ridges are smaller. The skeleton shows a stronger build than modern human but was well proportioned. All the hominids and homo fossils mentioned above are believed to the member of human family tree.

Australopithecus aethiopicus lived between 2.6 and 2.3 million years ago. This species is probably an ancestor of the robustus and boisei. This hominid ate a rough and hard to chew diet. He had huge molars and jaws and a bony ridge on the skull extending from the forehead to the back of the head. Massive chewing muscles were anchored to this crest. Brain sizes were still about 500cc, with no indication of speech functions. This hominid was mainly vegetarian that's why the brain size remained relatively small compared to meat eating hominid like *Homo habilis* and *Homo erectus*. Its descendant *Australopithecus robustus* had the small size brain due to same reason.

Australopithecus robustus lived between 2 and 1.5 million years ago. It had a body similar to that of *africanus*, but with a larger and more massive skull and teeth. Its huge face was flat and with no forehead. It had large brow ridges and a sagittal crest. Brain size was up to 525cc with no indication of speech capability. *A aethiopicus* and *A robustus* are not considered in the human family tree they are the side branch of the evolutionary tree..

Homo Neanderthal lived in Europe and the Mideast between 150,000 and 30,000 years ago. It is believed that

Homo erectus who migrated to Europe evolved into Neanderthals. They coexisted with Homo sapiens (archaic) and early Homo sapiens sapiens the modern man. They might have been killed off by the modern man. Recent DNA studies have indicated that the Neanderthal[43] was an entirely different species and did not merge into the Homo sapiens sapiens gene pool. Brain sizes averaged larger than modern human at about 1445cc but the head was shaped differently than modern man. His nose was large and was different from us in structure. He was a massive man at about 5'6" tall with an extremely heavy skeleton that showed attachments for massive muscles. He was far stronger than modern man. His jaw was massive and he had a receding forehead. But why they couldn't compete with the modern man? Close examination of the skull of modern human and the Neanderthal shows a slight difference. Researchers found that Neanderthals had a smaller larynx compared to modern humans and so they could not have produce various sounds like us, thus lagged behind in speech compared to us. The slight deficiency in intelligence and speaking power compared to the modern human was enough to push the Neanderthals out of existence. They buried their dead and took care their elders but no art work or decoration beads have been found in their caves as we find in the contemporary caves of modern human. This fact shows that he was definitely less intelligent than the modern man and that's why they lost the war with us[44].

Homo floresiensis is a species of dwarf humans discovered on the Indonesian island of Flores in 2003. It was only about 3feet in height and fully bipedal, with a very small brain size of 415cc. The skull has human-like teeth with a receding forehead and no chin. *Floresiensis* fossils which have been discovered belong to 38,000 to 13,000 years of age. It used stone tools and fire, and hunted pygmy elephants and the giant rats found on Flores island. Its discoverers believe that *floresiensis* is a dwarf form of *Homo erectus.* Dwarfism is very common on islands where large mammals like elephant evolve into a pygmy elephant equal to the size of a small cow.

The discovery of *Homo floresiensis* does not change the broad picture of human evolution, and certainly it was not our ancestor. Surely it is the most extreme case of human adaptation ever found, it suggests that humans are also subject to evolutionary forces as other animals. The fact that *floresiensis* lived so recently and yet has been unknown until now is very exciting, maybe there are some more surprises waiting to come out in our human family tree.

Fossil data suggest that modern humans evolved from archaic humans primarily in East Africa. A 195,000 year old fossil from Ethiopia shows the beginnings of the skull changes that we correlate with modern human, including a rounded skull case and a projecting chin. A 160,000 year old skull from Ethiopia also seems to be at the early stages of this transition. It had the rounded skull case but retained the large brow ridges of archaic humans. Somewhat more advanced transitional forms have been found in Tanzania dating to about 120,000 years ago. Early modern humans had expanded their range to South Africa by 115,000 years ago and into Southwest Asia about 95,000 years ago. Finally they did appear elsewhere in the World about 70,000 - 60,000 years ago.[44]

We know that *Homo erectus* left Africa nearly 2.4 million years ago settled all over Asia and parts of Europe. On the other hand, Neanderthals occupied Europe from 250 to 30 thousand years ago. Modern man replaced *H. erectus* and Neanderthal from Asia and Europe. How it happened is a big question which is still being debate. There are two hypothesis, first is "Out of Africa" and second is "Multiregional hypothesis".[44] According to second hypothesis the modern man evolved from Homo erectus in different geographical locations separately. But interbreeding with other population and the migrated African modern humans. This hypothesis has some weakness, because transitional fossils have not been found yet, like what we have found in Africa. Also more than a million years of separation between the populations is expected to have much more genetic difference between the races which we do not find.

According to the Out of Africa model, developed by Peter Andrews, modern Homo sapiens evolved in Africa about 200,000 years ago. Homo sapiens began migrating from Africa between 70,000 – 60,000 years ago and eventually replaced existing Neanderthal in Europe 30,000 years ago and Homo erectus in Asia about 60,000 years ago. Out of Africa has gained support from research using mitochondrial DNA. After analyzing genealogy trees constructed using 133 types of mtDNA,[45] researchers concluded that all humans were descended from a woman from Africa who lived around 100 thousand years ago.

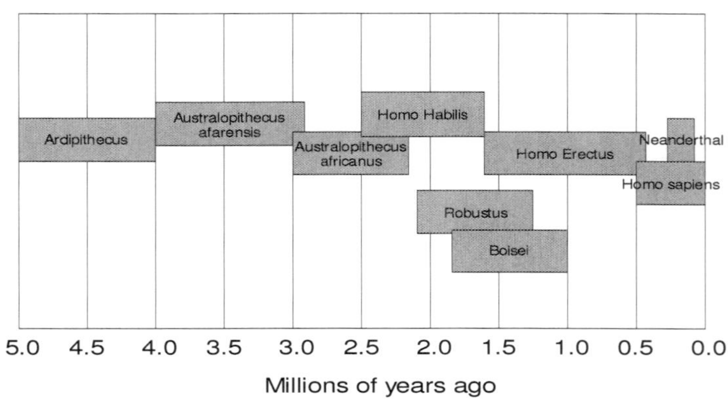

FIGURE 8. Shows time line relationship between the hominids.

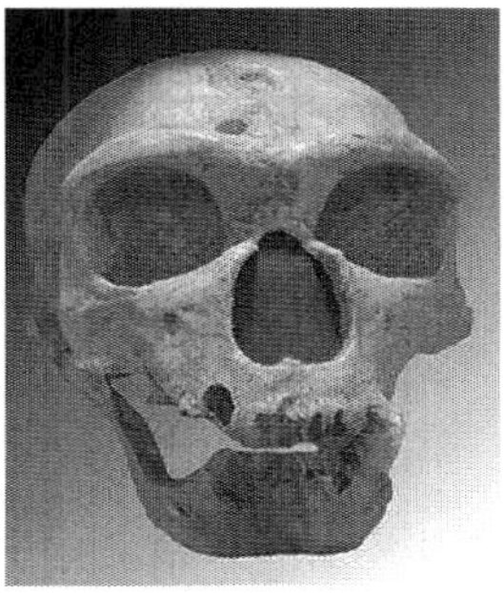

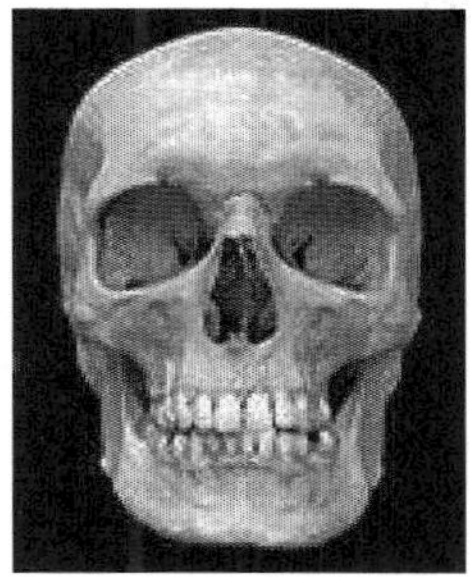

Neanderthal *Modern Human*

Homo habilis *Homo erectus.*

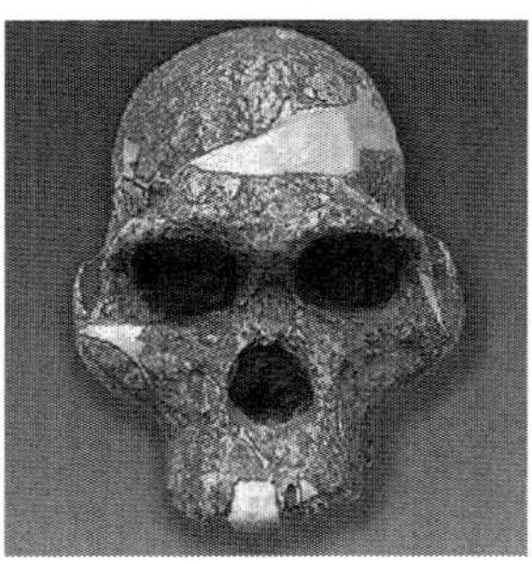

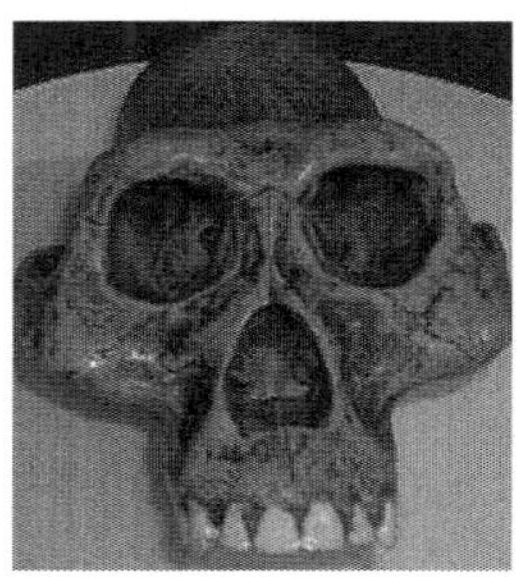

A africanus *A afarensis*

FIGURE 9 Fossils of Hominids and modern man

13

FINAL THOUGHTS

Now that you have read this far, I hope you are convinced by the evidence and the arguments presented in the chapters, that the theory of evolution is a fact. The evidence came from the fossil records found in geological time period in the same order as predicted by the theory of evolution. We never found any land living animal in a rock say 390 million years old. If we would have found even a single fossil out of place anywhere in the world, the theory of evolution would have collapsed. We discovered many transitional fossils in the layers of rocks as predicted by the theory. Out of 100 million fossils discovered, not a single fossil was found at a wrong geological stratum.

Predictive power of a theory is a powerful tool to verify its authenticity. The theory of continental drift predicts that the same kind of rock and fossil should be found on the east coast of South America and the west coast of Africa and we did. Now you can measure the drift by the GPS system which is about an inch a year. The theory of evolution predicts that we should find early hominid fossils on the African continent. And yes, all transitional fossils between humans and the great apes have been found in southern and eastern Africa. The theory of evolution predicted that a transitional fossil between fish and tetrapods should be found in rock about 375 million years old and we did. Numerous predictions like those mentioned above have turned out to be true.

Theory of evolution has been proven by the presence of vestigial organs in our own body and the body of other animals. The phenomenon of atavism also proves the theory, where humans in rare cases develop a tail, whales and the dolphins develops hind legs proving that their ancestors possessed those organs. Take the case of embryology and developmental biology, where an organism's evolutionary history is represented temporarily in its development stage. The human and fish fetus looks very similar at the initial stage. The human baby develops thick hair and tail at some stage of development only to disappear before birth. Almost all animals display the evolutionary history during their biological developmental stages. These events reminds us of our past evolutionary history.

Just like the theory of continental drift can be proved by the GPS system, the theory of evolution can be proved on molecular basis many times over. Gene similarity between the species, the degree of homology of nucleotide and amino acid among the species, cytochrome C similarity between the species, presence of pseudogenes in us and other creatures, immune responses between the species and DNA hybridization all proves evolution on a molecular basis. The new idea of epigenetic mark established only 15 to 20 years ago strongly supports the theory of evolution. You have seen bacteria evolving in laboratory setting and read all the time how bacteria are evolving to become resistant to antibiotics. Jerry Coyne author of book; *Why Evolution is True:* gives perfect summation of the situation:

> Every day, hundreds of observations and experiments

> pour into the hopper of the scientific literature… and every fact that has something to do with evolution confirms its truth. Every fossil that we find, every DNA molecule that we sequence, every organ system that we dissect supports the idea that species evolved from common ancestors. Despite innumerable possible explanations that could prove evolution untrue, we don't have a single one. We don't find mammals in Precambrian rocks, humans in the same layers as dinosaurs, or any other fossils out of evolutionary order. DNA sequencing supports the evolutionary relationships of species originally deduced from the fossil record. And, as natural selection predicts, we find no species with adaptations that benefit only a different species. We do find dead genes and vestigial organs, incomprehensible under the idea of special creation. Despite a million chances to be wrong, evolution always comes up right. That is as close as we can get to a scientific fact.

Newton's laws of gravity is excellent to find approximate results, but when there is a need for extreme precision, or when dealing with gravitation for *extremely* massive and dense objects, it fails. Newton's law of gravity has since been superseded by Einstein's theory of General Relativity which corrected the apparent discrepancy. Now Einstein's theory of relativity resists incorporation when it comes to quantum mechanics to form a cohesive model because general relativity is valid for a massive object only. It fails, when it comes to minute particles, so a new theory has to emerge to incorporate both massive objects and minute particles. No such thing has happened with the theory of evolution as a matter of fact the reverse is true. With the advancement in the science of molecular biology, biochemistry and genetics, the theory of evolution has established itself on a very solid ground so much so that among the qualified scientists and people it is an undeniable fact.

In spite of such overwhelming evidence for evolution there is a lot of resistance coming from religious organizations especially from Christian fundamentalists and other conservative groups. One conservative pundit, Ann Coulter writes in her bestselling book; *Godless: The Church of Liberalism*. She says:

> For liberal, evolution lets them off the hook morally. Do whatever you feel like doing – screw your secretary, kill your Grandma abort your defective child.

Ms. Ann Coulter ought to know that liberals have a much higher morality than conservatives. They are far better human being than them, because they feel the pain of the poor and unfortunate people. They not only care about the fellow human beings but all the creatures of the Earth because they believe we are all related. On the other hand the Christian conservatives think that they are the special creation of God. They have the right to subdue the Earth as preached by Bible. But how do you subdue the Earth? Cut the trees, kill the wild animals, exploit the natural resources of weak nations for profit and turn the weak people of another race into slaves.

Turn a few pages of American history and you will find that they were the conservative Christians of the south who were responsible for the cruel institution of slavery. They even fought a war with liberal north to save it. After the abolition of slavery they formed an organization called Ku Klux Klan to kill and terrorize the black minority. They were the conservative legislatures who voted against the Social Security Act, Medicare and now they are dead against health care reform, why, they don't feel the pain of the poor and don't want to share the wealth of this country with them. Twenty thousand poor people die in this country (USA) every year because they don't have the health care insurance. Who is responsible for their death? Who else? The pundit like Ann Coulter and her conservative associates. It was the neo-conservatives who were responsible for the unnecessary war in Iraq which resulted in deaths of hundreds of thousands of Iraqi people and more than four thousand deaths of our own young men. They don't mind spending trillion dollars on this useless war in Iraq but make a huge wave when it comes to spending money on health care reform, why, they don't feel the pain of the poor people.

Pat Robertson a Christian conservative pastor made the cruel remark that the earthquake in Haiti happened because the people of Haiti made a pact with the devil. In other words he is justifying the death and destruction of thousands of people as a punishment from God. How cruel you can be to make such a remark? He was chided by an atheist and a well known evolutionist Dr. Richard Dawkins for this cruel remark. Who has the higher morality? Pat Robertson or Richard Dawkin? He also collected large sums of money for the victims of earthquake.

Resistance for the idea of evolution is also coming from Muslim conservative groups. The Harun Yahya phenomenon-- the crusade against evolution is kind of new among Muslims. But he is not doing this on his own , he is heavily backed by Christian creationist groups of America. They think that through this campaign they will be able to introduce Christ in the Muslim world.[46] Taliban type Muslims are definitely against the idea of evolution. They are even against the modern education let alone the theory of evolution because of their utter ignorance and illiteracy.

Some educated Muslims also speak against evolution, they think by believing in evolution will weaken their faith which will be equivalent to committing a sin. In my opinion opposite is true, if God has created every thing through evolutionary process which has been proved as fact many times over, do you think that not accepting the truth will bring you closer to God? Denying the truth is to deny to God. Allama Iqbal the great poet and philosopher of the Indian subcontinent has said that modern science is compatible with Divine consciousness and that the scientific study of nature, which is what evolution is, brings man closer to God.

Some educated Muslims argue that believing in evolution will reduce our sense of morality and the law of the jungle will prevail. I say to them, that Hitler was a religious man he was not an atheist like Stalin. What sort of law prevailed in his regime? Most of the European countries whole heartedly embrace the theory of evolution yet they have managed to remain civilized. Unfortunately the law of jungle is prevalent in some of the Muslim countries who do not believe in evolution.

Things are not bad in the class rooms of Muslim countries. In fact, evolutionary biology is included in the curriculum of high schools of many Muslim countries including Pakistan where the relevant Qur'anic verses have been quoted in biology books. The quotations are not meant to contradict the idea of evolution rather to support it. The textbook of biology in Pakistan presents theory of evolution as a fact of science but the chapter on human evolution is missing from these textbooks without any comments.[47]

14

REBUTTALS

Four years ago when I came across Mr. Yahya's articles on evolution in The Muslim Observer, I thought that he must be a learned person and that's why I gave him some respect. But as time passed I learned more about him and found out that he is totally ignorant person. Here are some of the rebuttals.

I read with interest "The Miracles in Our Cosmos" the article written by Mr. Harun Yahya (Muslim Observer November 2006). He is a learned man and he has every right to believe and express his idea in public. But sometime in his crusade to derail the Darwin's theory of evolution, he has mentioned some facts which simply are not true. As a regular reader of *The Muslim Observer* I feel to discuss those facts one by one for the benefit of our readers.

In one of his article Mr. Yahya declared that the scientists have now rejected the theory of evolution and Darwin's idea has collapsed completely. This statement has no validity, and on the contrary there is overwhelming approval from the scientific community supporting the theory of evolution. With its explanatory and predictive power, this theory has become the central organizing principle of modern biology, relating directly to topics such as the origin of antibiotic resistance in bacteria and the staggering biodiversity of Earth's ecosystem. It was the sheer genius of Darwin that he put forward the theory of evolution at a time when all the natural science was in the state of infancy.

Jay Gould a Harvard professor explained that “evolution is a theory” and it is also a fact. So for the scientists the theory and fact do not stand in opposition, but rather exist in reciprocal relationship. An apple when dislodged from the branch of a tree will fall on the ground-- is a fact, which can be explained by the Newton’s theory of gravitation. In the same way, heritable variation, natural selection, response to selection (domesticated animals and plant) and the variation in the color of our own skin are facts which can only be explained by the theory of evolution. The modern theory of evolution is not just an idea of Darwin, its evidence is based on geological, morphological and molecular level. In one of the recent article Mr. Yahya says;

> Mutation do not cause living beings to develop; on the contrary, they are always harmful”

Let us examine what “mutation” is and how it affects the living organism. In biology mutation are changes to the genetic material (either DNA or RNA). Mutations can be caused by copying errors in the genetic material during cell division, by exposure to radiation, by chemicals (mutagens), and by viruses. In multicellular organisms, mutations can be subdivided into germline mutations, which can be passed on to descendants, and somatic mutations which cannot be transmitted to the descendants. Plants sometimes transmit somatic mutation to their descendants. Mutations creates variation in the gene pool, and the less favorable mutations are removed from the gene pool by natural selection, while more favorable ones tend to accumulate in given species. These changes in gene can accumulate over time due to genetic drift and can give rise to a new species. Thus we see how modern biology and chemistry has explained Darwin's concept of natural selection. Antibiotic resistant mutated bacteria is glaring example, it is bad news for us but good news for the organism. In the same article Mr. Yahya says;

> Although evolutionists have been making strenuous effort to find fossils since the middle of nineteenth century all over the world, no transitional forms (of Fossils)have been uncovered". He further writes "There should have existed some reptile-bird, which acquired some bird traits in addition to reptilian trait they already had.

I was amazed by this statement, because there are thousands of fossils of transitional from of species. The famous Archaeopteryx fossil found in 1861 at Bavarian limestone shows very clearly the link between dinosaurs and bird. More recently many such fossil have been found in China which are the perfect example of a transitional from between reptiles and bird.(See National Geographic vol. 194 July 1998). In the same way thousands of transitional fossils have been found showing the relationship between fish to amphibian, between amphibian to early reptiles, between reptiles to mammals and between non-human apes to modern humans. I can go on and on and fill all the space of *The Muslim Observer* with the names and characteristics of those transitional fossils which Mr. Yahya is looking for. In the face of such a overwhelming evidence it sounds so silly to say that life appeared on Earth all of a sudden and fully-formed.

I do not understand why creationists ignore the facts and insist that God created every life on earth, all of a sudden. No body can deny that God created every thing in the Universe. God also made the laws of the nature, and every thing is working according to His laws, then why will He not create all living things through His own laws? Qur'an says that God created every thing in stages and encourages us to go in nature and study it. What is wrong in finding the truth.

Evolution and the law of Thermodynamics.

Mr. Harun Yahya in his article 'The Secrets of DNA' (Muslim Observer, May 2007) argues that according to the Second Law of Thermodynamics the evolutionary process is not possible. He always makes the same mistake of providing the wrong information to prove his point. Let us discuss what he is trying to say in his article.

The Second Law of Thermodynamics can be defined in several ways, in a simple way it can be defined like this, "The entropy of a closed system cannot decrease." Entropy is a measure of the amount of disorder in a system. In most close systems the entropy (Disorder) tends to increase over time. This happens because of the fact that in a close system there is a limited amount of free energy, once that energy is used up to create order, it becomes unavailable for any further work and naturally the entropy will increase and the system will collapse. Creationists like Mr. Yahya thus misinterpret the Second Law of Thermodynamics to say that the system of evolution like any other system should also collapse. Here he neglected the fact that life is not a close system. The sun provides more than enough energy to drive any process. If a mature potato plant can have more usable energy than the seed it grew from, why should any one expect that the next generation of potatoes can't have more usable energy? Creationists like him try to get around this by claiming that the information carried by living things lets them create order. In nature order from randomness is very common in nonliving systems. Snowflakes, tornadoes, and lightning are just a few examples of order coming from randomness in nature. All these natural phenomenons require no intelligent program to achieve that order.

Mr. Yahya argues that even in an open system you need some sort of mechanism to convert the solar energy into chemical energy, like photosynthesis. He should know, that deep down in the ocean floor where there is no sun light, a special kind of bacteria drives the energy from hydrogen sulfide coming out of hot vents and supports a whole bunch of life. There is no photosynthesis going on at such a dark and deep ocean floor. This is a very recent discovery, which stunned the scientific community, because no body ever thought that life can exist without the aid of photosynthesis and in such an inhospitable environment. Mr. Yahya should understand that life can evolve even in the harshest condition if the source of energy and water is present, no matter, whether the source of energy is coming from a highly toxic gas, like hydrogen sulfide. This phenomenon is called chemosynthesis which further reinforces the theory of evolution.

His assertion that there is no natural mechanism to produce ordered life from disordered chemicals is simply not true. The unique chemistry of carbon atoms makes it possible for these atoms to use free energy (photons from the sun) to break and re-form chemical bonds and thus form long chains organic compounds; the genesis of the chemical basis for life. Nothing mysterious about this, it is simply a consequence of the laws of Chemistry and Physics (Made by God) as they apply to the atoms of carbon. These laws that govern the formation of biological molecules are the same that govern the formation of any other carbon compound. At the chemical level, there is nothing different about life; the chemistry of a carbon atom is the same whether that atom is part of a DNA molecule or whether it is part of an ordinary charcoal.

Dr. Yomlu is an eighty year old man of Turkish origin. One evening he came to the Canton Masjid to deliver a talk on the theory of evolution and about his own book.

I thank Dr. Yomlu for reading and taking interest in our articles and for his remarks published in *The Muslim Observer* on July 26, 2008. The main thrust of Dr. Yomlu's letter, as I see it, is to prove that the theory of evolution is not a scientific theory, rather it is just a belief. No sir, this theory is as sound as the theory of gravity, theory of continental drift or the theory of relativity. When Charles Darwin proposed the theory of Evolution, he almost did so in total ignorance of the disciplines we now know as genetics, cell biology, molecular biology, biochemistry, and paleontology. These branches of science have now gathered enormous amount of data that clearly support the theory of evolution. No scientific theory has been tested so thoroughly as the theory of evolution by thousands of brilliant scientists all over the world.

Dr. Yomlu has discussed about the randomness or disorder in nature, he believes every thing in nature is predetermined or in the state of order. His assertion that there is no natural mechanism to produce ordered life from disordered chemicals is simply not true. The unique chemistry of carbon atoms makes it possible for these atoms to use free energy (photons from the sun) to break and re-form chemical bonds and thus form a long of chain organic compounds-- the genesis of chemical basis of life, the first cell.

Deep down in the ocean floor where there is no sun light, a special kind of bacteria has evolved which drives the energy from hydrogen sulfide coming out of very hot vent (350c) and supports whole bunch of life. There is no photosynthesis going on at such a dark and deep ocean floor. Dr. Yomlu should understand that life can evolve even in the harshest condition if the source of energy and water is present.

Dr. Yomlu express the sense of surprise to see the verses from Qur'an in one of our articles. I say, why not? Qur'an strongly commands the believers to use his or her God given intelligence to understand the universe, its elements and the surroundings. The Qur'an says:

Say: Travel in the earth , then behold how Allah originated creation, then He produces a later creation: for Allah has power over all thing. (Qur'an 29:20)

There are other verses in the Qur,an which is clearly pointing towards evolution.

By the end of his long letter Dr.Yomlu is suggesting the reader to purchase his book for a more detailed discussion, which I did. I don't want make any comment about his book, but I shall have some remark about one chapter of his book, in which he has proposed a new theory of evolution based on quantum mechanics. He says;

> I am going to assume that: Species exist as a wave in blueprints, and as the wave collapses corresponding to a species, the species appears on this earth as a result. Included in this scenario are the first cell. microbes, plants, dinosaurs, ape and yes, even humans. As the waves collapsed (decohered) in virtual world they appeared here in the real world. It is like the scene in the TV show of Star Track, the captain is saying "Beam me up, Scotty". We can imagine each human organ such as heart, liver, kidney , brain and eyes are all available in the form of waves. Then the master plan assembles them

to produce a human being.

This is the abstract of Dr. Yomlu's New Theory of Evolution. Well, I could not figure out the head or the tail of his theory. I don't understand why he is still using the word '*evolution*' which he has condemned so much in his book; he should have used the title '*Wave Theory of Creation*' to present his bizarre idea, which he says is based on true science.

Genetic Closeness between Human and Chimpanzee

Mr. Harun Yahya in his article DNA Secrets (*The Muslim Observer* May 2007) declares that 98% similarity in genes between Human and Chimpanzee is a misleading propaganda. He portrays himself as a well educated scientist, but he is not afraid to mention completely wrong scientific information in his articles. He says:

> In order to claim that the genetic make-up of man and chimpanzee bear a 98% similarity the genome of chimp also has to be mapped, just like that of man, the two have to be compared, and the result of this comparison has to be obtained. However no such result is available, because so far only the human gene has been mapped. No such research has yet been done on the chimpanzee.

Mr. Yahya is either completely ignorant of the scientific work going on in this field or he is intentionally misleading about it. Contrary to his misinformation, chimpanzee's genes have been fully mapped by "International Consortium of Scientists" which includes the prestigious scientists from Harvard, MIT and Max Planck Institute of Evolutionary Anthropology. The result of the study has been published in Nature (September 1. 2005) and has

been compared with human genome. These are the people who have determined that 98.77 % genes are common in chimp and human, which Mr. Yahya is declaring as misleading propaganda. Time magazine (October 9, 2006) published an article "How we became human" mentions about this result which Mr. Yahya has conveniently ignored.
In another part of his article he quotes some funny research done at Cambridge University where according to him human beings and chickens were paired as the closest relative and that the next closest relative was crocodile. He is getting all this junk information to prove his point but he can't find the correct information. Mr. Yahya has every right to propagate his conviction under the freedom of speech, but he has no right Islamicly or otherwise to falsify the scientific facts to prove his point of view.

Rebuttal of Mr. Yahya's interview

I thank *The Muslim Observer* and Jams Adil for talking to this elusive writer Harun Yahya and publishing his long interview (TMO March, 2009). I say elusive because he is the only author I know who can't be reached directly by mail or e-mail. About two years ago, The New York Times was unable to make contact with him when he was sending his books to the professors of biology all over USA.

I don't know Mr. Yahya's educational background but I can say with confidence that he definitely does not understand biological evolution or science in general. He repeats like a parrot the same thing again and again that science and scientists have refuted evolution. I don't understand which science and scientist he is talking about. Evolution among the pseudo-scientists and flat earth enthusiast may be sitting on a shaky ground but among the educated scientists allover the world it is as solid as a rock. If the theory of evolution is a hundred page book, Darwin might have written its ten pages introduction, the rest of the book has been written by the modern scientists of almost all branches of science which include chemistry, biochemistry, biology, zoology, geology, paleontology, physiology and genetics. A scientific fact proven by all the branches of science can't be extinguished by name calling and chest beating and yes, opposing evolution is definitely opposing science which we Muslims can't afford. Mr. Harun Yahya in his interview has tried to mix science with religion when he asks this question:

> Can they account in terms of evolution for how the Prophet Musa's (as) staff turned into a fully formed snake with digestive, motor and reproductive systems when he threw it down on the ground. When the Prophet Jesus (as) breathed on a bird-shaped object made out of mud, it turned into a living, flying bird. How do they explain that?

No, no one can explain this scientifically or otherwise, neither Mr. Yahya can, because God does not do any thing that is against the universal laws which He has established Himself. Mr Harun Yahya ask this question:

> Why, if species have descended from other species by insensibly fine gradations, do we not everywhere see innumerable transitional forms? Why is not all nature in confusion instead of the species being, as we see them, well defined? Everything is highly regular and perfect".

Yes, Mr. Yahya, thousands of transitional fossils of different species have been found. Archaeopteryx is a glaring example which is intermediate between dinosaurs and birds, more recently many such fossils have been discovered in China. As a mater fact, you don't have to look for a for a fossil to prove that our regular chicken evolved from dinosaurs, because it still has genes of dinosaurs. For example, by manipulating the gene, teeth can be grown on chicken's beak and tale can be grown like a dinosaurs.

Of all the millions of species which Allah created on this Earth only 0.1% have survived to this day. If every species were formed well defined, and perfect as Mr. Yahya says, then why did 99.9% of God's creation become instinct? Well that's how God's plan works. God has grand plan, and with every changing condition on planet Earth a new species evolves to match that environment, the creatures which could not survive in that condition, simple becomes instinct. What could more simple and self sustaining than this system which Allah created ? Yahya ask this question;

> Evolution is a theory unable to explain even how a single protein came into being by chance, a theory at a complete dead-end.

First, he is asking this question to the wrong people. Evolution has nothing to do about how life came on Earth. Yes, chemist and biochemist have produced amino acids and proteins in laboratories from gases present in atmosphere when earth was young four billion years ago.

15

WHO IS HARUN YAHYA?

Harun Yahya, for some, is a Turkish writer who claims to have written many books ranging from scientific, faith-related ones to all of kinds political to social subjects and as a crusader against theory of evolution. Yet to others he is nothing but a charlatan, and a colon of Christian Creationist. I have read a lot about him but I have no comments to make. Read all these facts and make your own judgment.

Adnan Oktar (pen name Harun Yahya) was born in Ankara in the year 1956 where he finished his high school. In 1979 he moved to Istanbul to become an Interior Decorator but dropped out without completing the degree. He says in his book that he studied philosophy at Istanbul University but did not graduate over there either, so basically he has a high school diploma.

Edip Yuksel a famous Turkish writer and the former mentor of Yahya says in his article. Harun Yahya in his late twenties, a college dropout and unemployed was living with his mother in middle class neighborhood of Istanbul. In the early eighties he formed a cult and had some followers and by the late eighties he declared himself the promised Mahdi.

During the mid-eighties Henry Morris president of the Institute of Creation Research (ICR) and his son John Morris traveled to Turkey over a dozen times in search of Noah's Ark. Harun Yahya met Henry Morris which eventually led to the formation of Bilim Arastirma Vakif or BVA(Science Research Fondation) in 1991, an Islamic Creationist cell in Turkey. Duane Gish, Henry Morris (fonder of ICR) and his son John Morris visited Turkey in 1992 and participated in a Creationist conference in Istanbul[48]. After the conference Mr. Morris described the presence of the ICR in Turkey as an effort to bring Turks to Christ.[49] In another article, titled, "*Creation, Christmas, and the Qur'an*" Henry Morris hopes Muslims influenced by the ICR will come to know Christ. They are the same Morris who thinks that Prophet Muhammad (pbuh) was trafficking with the devil.[50] Mr. Yahya says he is doing the service to Islam but why he still closely associated with ICR, the Henry Morris's organization who has such a derogatory notion about our Prophet (pbuh)?

By the late nineties he started his crusade against the theory of evolution and published the book: *Evolution Deceit* and then on a host of books against Darwin and the theory of evolution . He claims to have written some 300 books, but being a high school graduate and a college dropout it is hard to believe that he is the writer of all those books. In fact Halil Arda, an investigative journalist in one of his articles has proved that he is not the author of the books he claims he has written[51], that is why some people call him a ghost writer. All his books refuting evolution are bunch of crap full of deceit and misinformations. The books and articles written against evolution is nothing but a copy of Christian creationist literature.[52] The arguments, the points and the subject matters are similar, except the word Christ has been replaced by Allah.

In 2007 he published an anti-Darwin magnum opus *Atlas of Creation,* 800 glossy pages with lavish illustration weighing more than 12 pounds. He distributed it unsolicited to ten thousand people including university professors both here in USA and Europe. According to New York Times the production cost of this book alone would run into more than a million dollars plus the cost of mailing. Many scientists who received the book, pondered, what to do with the book, for some it was too beautiful for the trash bin but too erroneous and full of garbage to keep on book shelves.[53] Professor Richard Dawkins derides the exercise as "total inanity" and says Yahya knows nothing about biology, science and about evolution he is trying to refute.[25]

In his book *Atlas of Creation* he has produced thousands of pictures of fossilized birds , snakes and other creatures side by side with there identical modern kin. He then argues that no change has taken place, so evolution is false. One of the pictures in the book which he has labeled as a Caddis fly is actually a man made fishing fly with a metal hook clearly visible. I have read this book myself and I came to the conclusion that it is nothing but a manifesto of deception and deceit.

Sometime in June of 2009 I was surfing the Internet to read about Harun Yahya, when I came across the reference of Amberin Zaman's article on Harun Yahya. I downloaded the article from a web site of Turkish Hurriyat magazine which has been blocked now by Harun Yahya. He has also managed to block some 70 web site for Turkish readers.

Amberin Zaman

Amberin Zaman is a well known journalist of Turkey, who writes articles for *The Los Angeles Times, The Economist of London* and *The Washington Post.* In one of her articles: *Police cracks down on obscure sect* published in *Turkish Hurriyat* she writes:

> When Ebru Simsek, one of Turkey's best known fashion models, went on a date with a handsome young businessman here five years ago, little did she know that she would come to regret accepting his offer for the rest of her life. Simsek, a curvaceous bottle blond, with striking blue eyes, thought she was going with her new boyfriend to a friend's birthday party. Instead, says Simsek she found herself at a villa overlooking the Bosporus Straits, drugged and naked with a gun pointed to her head. Like so many attractive, young women here, Simsek had been targeted by Adnan Oktar, (Harun Yahya) a self proclaimed Islamic cleric or imam who leads a, virulently anti-semitic sect known as the Science and Research Foundation. Duped by Oktar's businessman disciple Simsek was to have become the latest addition to his harem. "Oktar told me that unless I did as he bade I would be killed".

She had no choice but to become a part of his harem of fifty strong. Amberin paints Yahya as monster and she writes:

> Even the most hardened Islamists agree, however, that Oktar, (Harun Yahya), is a charlatan and that his arrest was long overdue. "He shamelessly used our holy Prophet and religion to enrich himself and indulge in the utmost degeneracy" said a prominent lawmaker from the Islam-based Virtue Party. The lawmaker, who asked not to be named said that he had been approached by various members of the sect several years ago.

According to the Amberin's article Harun Yahya's gang of 84 people were arrested by the Istanbul police in November of 1999. Most of his disciples were released after interrogation but Harun Yahya was locked up in jail for trail. He was charged for extortion, blackmail and sex with minors. Police recovered a huge number of pornographic video tapes showing a number prominent people like singers, politicians and rich businessmen in a very embarrassing situation. Ebru Simsek, the fashion model defected from Yahya's harem while he was in jail and reported to the police what happened to her. After his release from the jail Yahya punished Simsek by slandering her as a prostitute and sending her naked photographs to hundreds of newspapers and TV channels throughout Turkey.[51 54]

The judicial process which started after his arrest dragged on for two years and in the end the complainants retracted their charges. The case against Harun Yahya and other BAV members were dismissed at that time. Six year later another court picked up the cases again and in 2008 convicted Yahya and 17 other members for three years in jail on a variety of criminal charges.[55] He has appealed the conviction in the Supreme Court of Turkey.

Edip Yuksel

Edip Yuksel is a famous Turkish American writer. According to Wikipedia, he is considered one of the prime figures in the modern Islamic reform and "Qur'an Alone" movements. Author of many books on Qur'an and Islam, he has attracted much attention through his works and speeches. His main aim, as stated throughout his writings, is to spread an Islamic understanding that is rational, progressive, and humanistic, which in his eyes can only be gained through accepting the Qur'an as the Divine authority. He is also a promoter of theistic evolution, an understanding he gets from science and the Qur'an. His article on Harun Yahya is being published in this book with his consent. The author of this book have talked to him several times.

Harun Yahya: The Promised Mahdi?

By Edip Yuksel

The following article is mostly a personal attack. However, I am not committing the logical fallacy known as ad-hominem, since the attack is relevant to the argument and is justified. After reading the article, you will decide it for yourself.

Adan Oktar, who later started using the nickname Harun Yahya, was my apprentice in mid 1980's. In our first meeting, I was a famous Sunni author and political activist, and he was an unknown Sunni zealot influenced by the books of the Kurdish Mullah, Said Nursi. At that time, my books were making editions after editions and I had hundreds of thousands of readers, yet I had no special group of mine. He was not famous then, but he had a few dozen followers among university students. He was in his late twenties, a college drop-out, unemployed, and was living with his mother in an apartment located in a middle class neighborhood at Ortakoy, Istanbul. He had a long black beard, soft voice, smiling face, childish jokes, and most importantly a well calculated plan for his assumed mission.

Adnan Oktar (Yahya) was mixing mysticism with scientific rhetoric and presenting it gently and in a modern fashion to the children of the privileged class, without intimidating them. He was a refined and urbanized version of Said Nursi. Ironically, unlike beardless Said, he was fond of his well-groomed stylish beard. (Religious clerics, on the other hand, managed to grow ugly-looking beards by cutting their mustache short and shaving their hair, resembling Franciscan monks). This proved to be a magic solution. He would always keep a certain distance between himself and his followers and would treat them as if they were his children, though he was only seven or ten years older than them. He would pat the heads of his young pupils and encourage them to work for the mission and they would accept this charming and patronizing treatment with delight. He was targeting the university students, especially the handsome children of the rich and the affluent. They would pull each other to the circle.

Meanwhile, when I was doing my mandatory military service in Samsun in 1986, I started communicating with Rashad Khalifa. After several rounds of hot snail-mail discussions and upon reading his landmark book, *Qur'an, Hadith*, and *Islam*, I decided to dedicate my religion to God alone. I shared my newly discovered faith with my close friends, including Adnan Oktar. He was very receptive. He would frequently ask me questions and convey the information to his followers. He was trying his best to keep our meetings secret from his followers. Then I did not know the reason, and I did not care much. I thought he was considering my style too bold and my culture too rural. He was right: when discussing political or religious issues, I did not care much about people's clothes, wealth, or their personal feelings. But in retrospect I know the real reason behind this secrecy: he was thinking that my presence would jeopardize his charisma and dilute his influence over them. He wanted his followers to think that he was receiving special information or inspiration from God. He did not know Arabic but he was clever enough to dupe the unquestioning gullible followers and give them the impression that he knew a lot. He was considering me as a potential rival in his mission.

To my dismay, later I discovered that his interest in the message was not prompted by his philosophical quest for truth but by his pragmatic strategy for his political ambitions. He thought that he could use it easily to attract the children of the rich people who had modern life style and culture that was incompatible with the medieval Arab culture which was to be promoted by the teachings of Hadith and Sunnah. He was extremely obsessed with recruiting the handsome children of the rich people wearing expensive clothes. He was not interested in guiding poor people.

After discovering his intention and his deep belief that he was the promised Mahdi, I severed my relationship with him in 1988. Soon after this, he turned back to his Sunni roots . To expose his real face, I had secretly recorded one of my last conversations with him, but later I gave up releasing it. I just did not feel comfortable with the secrecy of my act. I had given the tape to Mustafa and Yelda Şahin, two of his former followers. However, after I was forced to immigrate and start a new life in America, I learned that the tape was handed to Girişim, an Islamic magazine directed by Mehmet Metiner. The magazine published the transcript to warn Sunni Muslims against Adnan's Machiavellian politics. In the taped conversation I was reprimanding him for cooperating with Sheikh Nazim of Cyprus who had influence among some wealthy British Muslims. He was apologetic and was justifying his relationship for purposes of using Nazim's influence. I warned him again for such tactics, since I always believed that honesty is a necessary characteristic of being a Muslim. The transcript of this conversation is available on the Internet and was also posted in Turkish forum of 19.org. A funny portion of the conversation reveals the appalling tactics used by Adnan Oktar to recruit members for his cult. In that portion I was criticizing him for preferring the wealthy.

Unveiling Adnan's secret relationship with me and his hypocrisy in his relation with Sunni leaders, in a normal world would mean that he too would be the target of a major attack, threats and excommunication. Surprisingly, despite this scandal, he continued to become a rising star in Sunni market. He was once secretly teaching his followers that Mustafa Kamal Ataturk was the prophesied Dajjal (deceptor) and later he embraced him for political reasons and declared him a great hero. He is now playing a double game: to appease the Turkish oligarchy he is exploiting Ataturk-worship, and to exploit the Muslim market he is indirectly giving the message that Ataturk was a disbeliever. He has played the game of double-speak pretty successfully so far. Adnan has danced among many contradictory positions, but the single conviction he has maintained since early 1980s is "Adnan Oktar is the promised Mahdi."

When I was trying to convince him about the message of the “Qur'an Alone” he did not insist nor even defended any traditional Sunni precepts, with the exception of Hadith about Mahdi. It amazed me for a short while to see him trying to strike a compromise with me regarding this issue. He wanted me to accept his conversion to the Qur'an Alone together with his belief about the promised Mahdi. I tried to tell him that the Hadith about Mahdi was among the most fabricated and unreliable Hadith, even according to the lousy standards of Hadith experts; they were fabricated by the supporters of Umayyad and Abbasid dynasties to promote the interest of the sultans. To him Mahdi (that is his leadership) was the most important subject. His take on Masons and Zionists is just a strategy to get him an international fame and popularity so that he may finally announce his mission to the world. His cult resembles the modus operandi of Moon or Scientology cult: targeting affluent people and exploiting their resources.

We met each other in prison too. In December 3, 1986 I was imprisoned second time for promoting a theocratic revolution in Turkey via the first volume of my best-selling book, *Interesting Questions*. Though I had written that book before my conversion from Sunni Islam to monotheistic Islam, the book was not reflecting my hard core revolutionary ideology; it contained some mild hints and innuendos. But, this was sufficient for the government to imprison me since (unaware of my radical transformation) they were trying to deter me from engaging in open and underground political activities.

I met Adnan (Harun Yahya) in the prison clinic. I was taken there by the doctor who happened to recognize me from my books and conferences; he wanted to save me from the crowded ward which was filled with convicted murderers and burglars. Adnan was there for a different reason, a much different one. He was acting like a paranoid schizophrenic in order to get medical report to dodge the draft. It was ironic, since he was indeed mentally sick; he was a delusional megalomaniac, yet he was cunningly acting for another mental illness. He was successful; he dodged the draft and since then he has been found lacking mental capability to be the subject of criminal law. So, he is getting away with sexual abuses, fraud, libel, blackmailing schemes, and other criminal activities. If Adnan Oktar has demonstrated a miracle as a Mahdi, this must be his miracle: he is officially insane and criminally Teflon!

Though Adnan (Harun Yahya) is a lay person by academic standards, he is a gifted manipulator, a patient and highly skilled team manager: he uses various highly efficient psychological devises and marketing gimmicks to depict his image as a divinely ordained leader with a great mission. It would be in the best interest of the naive and young pupils to join his cause, since soon he will be ruling the entire world and they would be his lucky and powerful aids. Besides, the cult provides a holy club for the children of the rich and the well connected; they also get second-hand girls as a fringe benefit. In turn they lose their freedom and part of their identity; but we know that millions of people are ready to trade those precious rights and values to join a cult or a religious organization. Though the dates for victory he has given have been extended several times, who would not be the secretary or the spoke person of the long-awaited great ruler of the entire world? If it is not in 1999, then the victory would come in 2005, or in 2014. The Jehovah Witnesses have extended the end of the world several times in a century, and Adnan, as I know him, is no less talented than them. After his death, his followers will have enough experience to keep the enthusiasm of the army of the Mahdi until the end of the world. An army comprising of rich, educated and devoted cult members who are experts in cutting and pasting, clipping and editing, in putting together the plagiarized pieces like a jig saw puzzle, and are generous in presenting them to masses under the name of their leader, yes this army is a powerful force. But, there is always the risk of getting into a holy fight for leadership after the Mahdi.

Adnan's relation with me became the topic of articles and political analyses in Turkish media, books and magazines (for instance, see Ayet ve Slogan by Ruşen Çakır, a prominent Turkish journalist), and his frequent turns and twists have been well documented in Turkish media, such as Hurriyet, Milliyet, Radikal, Sabah newspapers. Many of his followers left him with disappointment; but each time a group left him, he was somehow able to maintain his cult by attracting fresh blood from gullible youth ready to become the future rulers of the globe as Mahdi's close assistants. His former followers were intimidated and blackmailed in sophisticated ways and occasionally in Mafia style. They work like a professional intelligence agency with covert operations and misinformation campaigns. Their habit of getting what they want via blackmail, slander and libel put them in trouble with high ranking Turkish politicians several years ago. As I said above, Adnan Oktar showed his miracle: his medical report regarding his mental illness not only saved him from mandatory military service but also from the criminal prosecutions.

Adnan Oktar is not formally educated, neither in science nor in religion, and he is not capable of understand in depth of subjects that are presented in books and videos carrying his nick name. Therefore, you never see him in public debating with experts. A single public discussion on a TV channel would be enough to turn him to the proverbial Naked King. And he may consider this article as my challenge for him: I am ready to meet him in a live debate on TV.

Adnan Oktar uses proxies and gets credit for everything. He uses his medical report and gets away form any criminal charge. There are a lot to learn from Adnan Oktar or the exploiter of the names of two messengers of God, Harun and Yahya. His followers, mostly educated and rich, yet gullible youngsters, work day and night to prepare books and videos mostly plagiarized from works of western scientists and artists. In the end, those collaborative and plagiarized works are all together credited to Harun Yahya. Thus, Harun Yahya is a brand name, an artificial name aimed to boost the personal agenda of Adnan Oktar, a pathetic megalomaniac. For instance, in 1990's many of the books credited to him were written by his former follower Metin Kımıldar who also used the nick name Cavit Yalçın. Where are you Cavit Yalçın now? Are you now renting your nick name as a portal for Harun Yahya's websites or is it taken away from you?

Adnan Oktar is the most cunning charlatan and master human manipulator I have ever witnessed. He strongly believes that he is the Mahdi (the Sunni and Shiite imitation of Messiah) and he has the manipulative charisma, the pool of unlimited gullible rich people and a market of more than a billion individuals easily impressed by the work of his followers.

Knowing him before 1990s, I could not believe that he would be indulging in promiscuous sexual activities, since at that time he was a devout Sunni who was very scrupulous about interacting with women. He would not even shake hands with women. However, with time, Adnan Oktar evolved and was transformed. His sexual abuse of girls around him has been the frequent topic of Turkish media and acknowledged by the defectors. He claims the right to have sexual intercourse with every female member of his cult. He has even invented a name for those females: motor (engine). Reportedly, his male followers are feeling lucky in letting him taste their girl friends first.

For recruiting new members and promoting his brand name, he uses sex, money, popular symbols, and famous people. But the main tool he uses is deception, yet I think he does the deception "righteously", that is for a good end. He justifies his deceptive propaganda by the abused Quranic word Taqiyya (this holy hypocrisy is a part of belief system of Shiite sect) After learning Rashad's claim of messenger ship and his argument regarding the definition of Rasul and Nabi, Adnan assumed to be a messenger and expressed this belief to his closest circle. I think later, to be able to access the one billion Muslim market, he went back to his original claim of Mahdi. There he could exploit to the bone. But, his picking Harun Yahya as his nickname indicates his deep belief in his messenger-ship. Why? Well, here is a clue: because of his ignorance of the Qur'an, he thinks that Harun was not given any book, so according to him Harun was a messenger but not a prophet.

It is a shame to see modern Muslims are duped by this charlatan. These books and videos are mostly plagiarized collections of western work that mixes truth with falsehood. Science is mixed with pseudo-science, such as ignorant criticisms of the theory of evolution. The message of the Qur'an is mixed with fabricated Hadith, such as the identity and adventures of the Mahdi. Looking at the popularity and success of this charlatan, if I was gullible enough to believe in Hadith narrations, I would be impatiently waiting for the Mahdi against this Dajjal.

Halil Arda

New Humanist is the London based magazine of the Rationalist Association promoting free thought since 1885. In September/ October issue of 2009 I found a very comprehensive article on Yahya: *Sex, flies and videotape the secret lives of Harun Yahya* written by Halil Arda an eminent journalist. This article is a masterpiece of investigative journalism. Arda writes:

> Inspired by the high profile of its Christian American counterpart, Muslim creationism is becoming increasingly visible and confident. On scores of websites and in dozens of books with titles like The Evolution

Deceit and The Dark Face of Darwinism, a new and well-funded version of evolution-denialism, carefully calibrated to exploit the current fashion for religiously inspired attacks on scientific orthodoxy and "militant" atheism, seems to have found its voice. In a recent interview with The Times Richard Dawkins himself recognizes the impact of this new phenomenon: "There has been a sharp upturn in hostility to teaching evolution in the classroom and it's mostly coming from Islamic students."The patron saint of this new movement, the ubiquitous "expert" cited and referenced by those eager lie", is the larger-than-life figure of Harun Yahya.

Halil Arda wonders:

How did such a man acquire the standing, and the financial resources, to be a player in global debates about the origins of life and the future of relations between Islam and the West? To answer this I have traveled repeatedly to Istanbul over the last few months (at my own expense), contacting sources and speaking to former members of his group, to journalists and political commentators who have followed his bizarre career and to legal experts who have defended individuals targeted by Yahya's organizations. Many of my interviewees spoke on condition of anonymity, out of fear of the barrage of court cases his defectors and critics have been facing in recent years, described by one of his former acolytes as a campaign of "legal terror".

While Oktar was building a public profile through his books, the real work was taking place backstage, as he began to assemble a group of followers dedicated to his twisted vision. Combining his undoubted charisma (something even his most ardent opponents concede) with a gift for manipulation, Oktar set out to build a cult around himself, drawing extensively on the techniques pioneered by messianic gurus like Charles Manson and Jim Jones, and in particular employing the strategies of the Moonies, the Bhagwan Shree Rajneesh and Scientology in targeting disaffected but affluent and educated young people, insisting they turn their worldly goods over to the cult, and vigorously enforcing rigid hierarchies and punitive rules.

Though, as with all cults, it is extremely hard to understand what draws young, rich and educated people in, Dilek, a former follower of Oktar, gives something of the flavor. Now a suave businesswoman in her late 30s, Dilek remembers how she first met Oktar, visiting him while he was still in mental hospital, after her then boyfriend had turned out to be a follower. "I was expecting someone who frightens you off, someone terrible," she told me. "He was the opposite. He was tall, with rosy cheeks and blue eyes. He was laughing a lot, he was full of love." She was seduced.

On his release Oktar began to hold meetings in cafés and private residences in Istanbul's posh suburbs, where a growing number of rich and beautiful young people gathered for debate and prayer. Soon Dilek donned a headscarf, but only outside her parents' house, so as not to alert them to her new-found religious commitment. All her friends in the group were graduates of expensive public schools, educated in foreign languages, and most were the children of rich families and many of well-known personalities. Such "awareness-raising" meetings and discussion groups are part and parcel of Islamist group mobilization. Yet Oktar's group soon took a different turn. "Suddenly Adnan Hodja repudiated all oral traditions relating to the words and deeds of Muhammad (Hadith) and decided that the Koran would be the only point of reference," says Dilek. "Henceforth, he reduced the five daily prayers to three, and he dropped the veiling of women. He told us the Mehdi would emerge from Turkey, and he would come with an army of youth. He never said that he was the Mehdi himself, but we all believed that he was."

Throughout the 1980s and early '90s, Oktar built up his community. Followers were especially active in the swanky summer resorts along the shore of the Sea of Marmara. A friend of mine, who spent most of her holidays in the late 1980s at her parents' summer flat in the area, recalls how the followers' targeting worked: "They bought flats there and singled out attractive girls and boys. The boys were very good-looking, boys who can easily charm you. I guess this is why they started with the boys. Once the girls entered the cult, they had to give up sexy fashion, so they wouldn't be able to attract new members. But for the boys, the rules were more relaxed, so that they could continue recruitment."

The social organization within the group was becoming rigidly hierarchical and, as is common in messianic cults, sexual relations were tightly controlled, with the putative messiah given access denied to others. Oktar considered all female members his legitimate possession. Berk, a recent defector after seven years, describes the groups: "There were sisters (bacilar), concubines (cariyeler) and brothers (kardesler), the male members. The brothers were allowed to marry the concubines, while the sisters were all married to Adnan Oktar." Of course these marriages were not legal, but they were treated as such within the group. As with Scientology, discipline was maintained through humiliation, the threat of expulsion and physical violence. I know personally, Berk told me, that Oktar beats the sisters.

Okatr also insisted on uniformity in dress, behavior and even home furnishings. "Everyone had to be the same," says Berk. "The hairstyle, the shoes, the jackets. It had to be the most expensive brands, like Versace and Gucci, and it had to be exactly how he wanted it to be. Even our communal flats had to be furnished according to his taste. It had to be heavy antiques, all with gold leaf and dark wood." Video cameras were installed in the communal apartments, which allowed Oktar to exercise

> control over his followers and outsiders. As the criminal indictment vividly illustrates, young girls were lured into sex parties with the promise of being admitted to the group, but ended up having to perform sexual acts with men of influence, whom the group needed for its economic and political success. The encounters were filmed and used to coerce the men in question to act in the group's interest. In witness statements, the models Tugce Doras and Seckin Piriler give detailed accounts of how members of the group treated them as "sex slaves" and how Oktar and his followers compelled them to perform oral sex and other sexual favors.

Halil Arda explains how Harun Yahya kept his followers in line by misinformation about Qur'an, Islam and the Islamic history.

> No matter how bizarre the rules, Oktar was able to provide them with apparent legitimacy through his reading of the Qur'an and Islamic history. Concubinage was justified by reference to the Ottoman harems, while passages of the Qur'an were recited to justify the practice of severing the ties of the young followers to their families. As a leading legal scholar involved in some of the court cases against Oktar(Harun Yahya) puts it: "In Oktar's reading, the love for mother and father is an offense to God. Parents are seen as the executors of God's will to raise the child. Once the child reaches adulthood, their role is fulfilled. If the parents happen to join, they are considered pious and may become fellow comrades. If they remain infidels, they are considered enemies." It was with this justification that the followers cut off relations with their parents, on whose financial and social resources, however, the group ultimately depended. The indictment details the way in which followers were encouraged to plunder their parent's bank accounts and sell their assets.

Halil Arda finds out the truth about book writing.

> It is highly doubtful whether any of books he claims to have written – were actually written by Adnan Oktar. Berk, who was part of the inner circle at the time, confirms this: "There is a group of followers who are commissioned to write the books. For every book, they will take a few key sources written by Christian creationist authors, mostly from the US. They plagiarize the chapters and paragraphs that agree with their creationist approach. Then they add the photos, a few ayat from the Qur'an, and sometimes a bit of a commentary. None of the ideas belong to Oktar. "
>
> Oktar's ideological and political promiscuity seem to support the claim that he has no genuine beliefs at all, and merely opportunistically jumps on issues which will further his notoriety, following the lead of smarter followers. As one former follower told me, "We had something to please everybody: Ataturk, Namaz (prayer), creationism and, if need be, cocaine."

Halil Arda hints that the Harun Yahya cult may be in decline, he writes:

> But with so many ideas taken up and discarded, and their leader facing jail, might the group be nearing exhaustion? True, the Science Research Foundation and the followers have initiated thousands of court cases. Three hundred alone were brought against the model Ebru Simsek, who spoke out against Oktar, a barrage of faked naked photos of her were made public. Oktar's followers have shot thousands of compromising videos of everyone who has come into intimate contact with the group. They have intimidated prosecutors, judges and lawyers with endless streams of complaints and faxed denunciations and printed libelous advertisements in the Islamist media, defaming their critics. They been especially effective on the Internet, setting up numerous websites to denounce their enemies, while using the Turkish courts to silence them – the Dawkins site is just

> one of dozens they have had banned. "They may be only a few hundred people," one lawyer told me, "but the damage they have inflicted is considerable. Damage to the families, to the judicial system, and to Turkish politics."
>
> And there may be deeper, structural reasons for the group's decline. In the late 1980s, after several babies were born to group members (whether Oktar's or not is unclear), Oktar forbade sexual practices that would lead to pregnancy (his followers were limited to anal or oral intercourse). Since then there have been no more births in the group. Anecdotal evidence suggests that Oktar's formerly aggressive recruitment has abated, too.
>
> What remains is a closed community of broken individuals. Berk, who has had to endure his fair share of slander and court cases, nevertheless feels compassion for his former comrades: "You have to understand that these are people who have sold everything they had; they sold what their parents had. They possess nothing. Many are now in their late 30s and 40s. They have lost their families and their social networks, and they have lost the ability to socialite. The only thing they know is to talk about Adnan's distorted version of Islam." Dilek, who broke with the group a few years ago, left two sisters behind. Her family sees them once or twice a year, when they visit guarded by a group of brothers. "They are like zombies," she told me. "As if there is nobody inside."

Halil Arda concludes how this empty man gained the prominence he has.

> Clearly Oktar is a master of manipulation, a "cunning charlatan" as Edip Yuksel calls him, but it is not this alone that has allowed this deluded, empty man to achieve the prominence he has. He is a symptom of our own sickness. Thanks to the "War on Terror", Oktar could paint himself as a credible alternative to radical Islam; thanks to our timidity and incompetence around

issues of faith he can gain credibility as a representative of Muslim sentiment and a champion of "inter-faith dialog". And, most of all, for many disoriented Muslims, he provides a compelling vision of a superior Islamic science.

He is a deluded megalomaniac who has artfully exploited the global resurgence of religious sentiment to cheat us all. A ludicrous man for ludicrous times.

REFERENCE

1. Charles Darwin, *The Origin of Species* p. 28
2. MacGregor, A.J., 1985. *The Impacted Lower Wisdom Tooth*, Oxford University Press, New York, p. 3
3. Ebbert, S. and Sangiorgio, M., 1991. *Facing the dreaded third molar.* Prevention, 43(7):1
4. Conway Zirkle, 1941, Natural Selection before the *'Origin of Species'* American Philosophical Society 84 p. 71
5. *Tusi's Views on Evolution*, Azerbaijan International, Internet.
6. Pervez Hoodbhoy, *Islam and Science, 1991, p. 57*
7. Allama Iqbal, *Reconstruction of Religious Thought in Islam*, p 45.
8. Hossein al-Jisr *Falsafa, Science and Qur'an* p. 203 to 211
9. Dr. Hamidullah, *The Emergence of Islam*, 1993 Islamic Research Institute, Islamabad
10. John Herlihy, *Modern Man at the Crossroads*
11. Biruni, Al (1000 CE) Athar-Ul-Bakiya , Translated by Dr. C Edward Sachu, p.98

12. Dalrymple, G. Brent, 2001 *The age of the Earth in the twentieth century,* Special Publications, Geological Society of London

13. Washington Post September 5, 2005

14. Eva Jablonka , Marion J. Lamb *Evolution in Four Dimensions,* Genetic, Epigenetic, Behavioral, and Symbolic Variation in the History of Life .

15. T.Cavalier-Smith (1987) *The origin of eukaryote and archaebacterial cells*, Annals of the New York Academy of Sciences

16. Cavalier-Smith (2002) *The neomuran origin of archaebacteria*, International Journal of Systematic and Evolutionary Microbiology 52, 7–76

17. Jerry A. Coyen 2009 *Why Evolution is true* Viking Penguin p. 52

18. Neil Shubin 2008 *Your Inner Fish* p. 40

19. Stewart J. R. (1997): *Morphology and evolution of the egg* Academic Press, London

20. Steven M. Stanley, *Earth System History* W. H. Freeman and Company, 1999)

21. Don E. Wilson & DeeAnn M. Reeder (editors). 2005. *Mammal Species of the World.* A Geographic Reference (3rd ed), Johns Hopkins University Press

22. Rose, Kenneth D. (2006). *The beginning of the age of mammals,* Baltimore: Johns Hopkins University Press.

23. Charles Darwin 1871 *Descent of Man, p.161*

24. Neil H. Shubin and Farish A. Jenkins, April 2006. *A Devonian tetrapod-like fish and the evolution of the tetrapod body plan,* Nature 440

25. Wall Street Journal, March 12 2009

26. Nishikimi, M., R. Fukuyama, et al. (1994) Mapping of the human nonfunctional gens. Journal of Biological Chemistry 269: 13685-13

27. J.H. Marden, Holler, *A respiratory hemocyanin from an insect.* Proceedings of the National Academy of Sciences 101: 871-874.

28. Gary Haynes, *Mammoth, Mastodon and Elephant* Cambridge University Press 1991

29. Jeheskel Shoshani *Elephants* Hardcover, Simon & Schuster, Limited

30. Philip D. Gingerich, D. E. Russell (1981), *Pakicetus inachus, a new archaeocete,* Univ. Mich. Contr. Mus. Paleontology 25: 235–246.

31. Mead, James G. and Robert L. Brownell, *Mammal Species of the World.* Johns Hopkins University Press, 2006

32. Muller, G. B. (2002) *Vestigial Organs and Structures,* in Encyclopedia of Evolution. Mark Page, editor in chief, New York: Oxford University Press.

33. Andrews, R. C. (1921) *A remarkable case of external hind limbs in a humpback whale,* Amer. Mus. Novitates. No. 9. June 3, 1921

34. Gilbert, S. F. (1997) *Developmental Biology.* Fifth edition. Sinauer Associates.

35. Strahler, Arthur, *Amino acid sequences in cytochrome c proteins from different species,* Science and Earth History, 1997

36. Charles Sibley, Jon Ahlquist, *The Phylogeny of the Hominoid Primates, as Indicated by DNA-DNA Hybridization".* Journal of Molecular Evolution .

37. Kinoshita, S.; Kageyama, S., Iba, K., Yamada, Y. and Okada, H. (1975),*Utilization of a cyclic dimer and linear oligomers of e-aminocaproic acid* Agricultural & Biological Chemistry 39 (6): 1219–23

38. The Washington Post October 2, 2009

39. Donald Johanson, *Ancestors, In Search of Human Origins* Random House Inc. 1981

40. Nitecki, M.H. and D.V. Nitecki (eds.). 1994. *Origins of Anatomically Modern Humans.* New York. Plenum Press.

41. Jia, Lanpo, Huang, Weiwen. *The Story of Peking Man: From Archaeology to Mystery.* Oxford University Press, USA, 1990

42. Smith, F. H., F. Spencer (eds.), 1984, *The Origins of Modern Humans*

43. Langaney A, Chech M, et al. (2004) *No evidence of Neandertal mtDNA contribution to early modern humans,* Journal, Paleobiology.

44. Donald Johanson *Origins of Modern Humans* Multiregional or Out of Africa, Internet

45. Cann, R.L., M. Stoneking, and A.C. Wilson. 1987, *Mitochondrial DNA and human evolution.* Nature, 325:32-36

46. Institute of Creation Research *ICR publication, Impact* # 318 December 1999

47. Punjab Textbook Board, Biology 12, Lahore Pakistan.

48. Harun Yahya, *Evolution Deceit*

49. ICR publication, *"Back to Genesis"* December 1998, page 120

50. Henry M. Morris, *The Long War Against God*, Grand Rapids, Michigan: Baker Book House 1989, pp. 229-30).

51. Halil Arda, *New Humanist*, October 2009

52. Cloning Creationism in Turkey, National Center for Science Education. Wikipedia

53. The New York Times, July 17, 2007

54. Mukto Mona, *Who is Harun Yahya,* Wikipedia

55. Reuters, May 9, 2008

INDEX